BEST NERDS FOREVER

James Patterson is the internationally bestselling author of the highly praised Middle School books, *Katt vs. Dogg*, *Ali Cross*, and the Treasure Hunters, Dog Diaries and Max Einstein series. James Patterson's books have sold more than 400 million copies worldwide, making him one of the biggest-selling authors of all time. He lives in Florida.

Chris Grabenstein is a *New York Times* bestselling author who has collaborated with James Patterson on the I Funny, Jacky Ha-Ha, Treasure Hunters, and House of Robots series, as well as *Word of Mouse*, *Katt vs. Dogg*, *Pottymouth and Stoopid*, *Laugh Out Loud*, and *Daniel X: Armageddon*. He lives in New York City.

Charles Santoso loves drawing little things in his little journal and dreams about funny, wondrous stories. He is the creator of Happy Hippo and has illustrated many books, including the *New York Times* bestseller *Wishtree* by Katherine Applegate and *Ida, Always* – a picture book written by Caron Levis, which was mentioned in the *New York Times* as 'an example of children's books at their best'. He moves around between different countries to live and work. You can visit him at www.charlessantoso.com.

BEST NERDS FOREVER

JAMES PATTERSON
AND CHRIS GRABENSTEIN

ILLUSTRATED BY
CHARLES SANTOSO

1 3 5 7 9 10 8 6 4 2

Young Arrow
20 Vauxhall Bridge Road
London SW1V 2SA

Young Arrow is part of the Penguin Random House group of companies
whose addresses can be found at global.penguinrandomhouse.com

Penguin
Random House
UK

First published in Great Britain by Young Arrow in 2021

www.penguin.co.uk

A CIP catalogue record for this book is available from the British Library

ISBN 9781529120066

Printed and bound in Great Britain by Clays Ltd, Elcograf S.p.A.

The authorised representative in the EEA is Penguin Random House Ireland,
Morrison Chambers, 32 Nassau Street, Dublin D02 YH68

MIX
Paper from
responsible sources
FSC   FSC® C018179
www.fsc.org

Penguin Random House is committed to a sustain-
able future for our business, our readers and our
planet. This book is made from Forest Stewardship
Council® certified paper

BEST NERDS FOREVER

CHAPTER 1

GREAT. YOU'RE HERE. I might as well get this whole messed-up story off my chest.

On June sixth, right before I was about to finish middle school, I was out riding my Tony Hawk bike, which my parents never liked because, come on—Tony Hawk. That maniac started skateboarding when he was nine years old. You ever seen the moves he makes in his video game? Extremely dangerous.

I love them, but my parents aren't big risk-takers. That's why my bike was neon orange. My mother wanted people, specifically drivers, to be able to see me from half a mile away.

Except that didn't exactly work.

It's after school. Maybe four-thirty in the afternoon. I'm riding my bright-orange bike up, down, and around Ridge Rim Road. Just cruising. Psyching myself up for the big hill I know is coming.

All of a sudden, I hear this engine roaring behind me. I mean, the driver's gunning it.

I shoot a quick look over my shoulder.

Here comes a HUGE rattling black van. It looks like the driver is aiming straight for me. I pump my legs. Pedal harder. Ride really, really fast.

The van picks up speed, too. Its engine is screaming. It's like I'm being chased by some super-creepy clown straight out of a Stephen King horror movie, which, as it turned out, I kind of was.

I can't figure out what to do because all I can think about is how the van might be trying to kill me. Seriously. When the driver saw me and my bright-orange bike, I swear they floored the gas pedal.

So, of course, I'm terrified. (You ever been chased by a demon van? It's very terrifying stuff.)

I work my legs so hard it feels like my thigh muscles might explode and burst into flames.

We're racing straight up a very steep hill. And, in the high-stakes road version of rock, paper, scissors, van always beats bike.

I can hear that motor whining behind me. It's getting closer. Closer. I can smell burning oil. I can almost feel the heat blasting out of the radiator grille. Its front bumper is nearly nudging my rear tire. The maniac wants to run me off the road!

I decide to ditch in some bushes I see on the shoulder. Sounds like the smart thing to do, right? Nope.

Very bad move.

Those shrubs are masking something: a low stone wall acting as a guardrail. My front tire slams into it. I go flying over the handlebars.

And I plummet off a cliff.

Oh—did I mention, there's a whole pile of sharp, craggy rocks a hundred feet below?

Well, there is. Trust me. I know. I died on them.

Yep. If you squint, you can see my bike down there.
It's bright orange. It also looks like a pretzel.
A bright-orange twisted pretzel.

3

CHAPTER 2

I KNOW, I KNOW, I KNOW—you weren't expecting me to die so soon.

Me, neither.

Anyway, I've never died before so I'm not exactly sure what I'm supposed to do.

I—or my soul or spirit or whatever—just sort of hang out down on those jagged rocks. My first reaction is "Whoa," because I look up and see how far I've fallen. We're talking a long, long, *long* way. Enough to make me sick to my stomach.

You might be wondering if, back when I was being chased, I memorized the demonic van's license plate number. Well, no, I did not. In fact, I only looked over my shoulder that one time. I was panicking, remember? Plus, even if I did know my killer's license plate number, what good would it do me? I'm dead. I can't really go running to the nearest police station to file a complaint or whatever.

And you're right. Seconds ago, I was up on Ridge Rim

Road looking *down* at my mangled bike so how can I, all of a sudden, be standing next to it looking *up*? I have absolutely no idea. I'm clearly new at this being dead thing.

I start thinking about movies I've seen about dead people. (I watch a lot of movies.) I expect to see a tunnel of light because, in the movies, there's always a tunnel of light you're supposed to walk into after you die. Usually, it's filled with ancient ancestors who help you move on. I think they call them guide spirits.

But the thought of bumping into some distant aunts, uncles, or cousins—ones I might not even remember or know—makes me a little nervous. Did I send enough thank-you notes to these dead people while they were still alive? Or will they be all like, "Oh, look who's here. It's Finn. The boy who never thanked me for that five-dollar bill I slipped into his birthday card. . .*eight years ago*!"

Oh, in case you were wondering, the van that chased me off the cliff never turned around to see what it had done. My hit-and-run driver showed absolutely no remorse. Psychopaths driving demonic vans straight out of a Stephen King movie seldom do.

But one thing I notice for maybe the first time? How great the pine trees smell along Ridge Rim Road. I've ridden up that hill a thousand times but never once smelled the trees. Now, the pine scent is kind of spectacular. Like Christmastime at my best friend Christopher's house. His family always brings home a real evergreen tree. And it always smells way better than the pine-scented air freshener we use at my house to make our fake tree seem less, you know, fake.

After a while, I start feeling guilty. I mean, why'd I have to go and die in a place where nobody ever goes, especially when looking for dead people? Ridge Rim Road is sort of close to the Lake, but nobody drives on it much (except, you know, demented psycho van drivers).

I try screaming anyway.

"Little help down here! Hello???"

I don't think my ghostly attempt at yelling made much sound. A bird chirping in a nearby tree did stop singing for a second and tilt its head slightly sideways. Did it hear me? Two seconds later, it's cheerfully chirping again so who knows.

The bird's happy.

Me? Not so much.

CHAPTER 3

I KNOW MY PARENTS will start worrying pretty soon.

It's getting close to dinnertime and we have a very rigid meal schedule at my house. Dad walks in the door at precisely five-twenty-two every evening. Then we all sit down to dinner at precisely five-thirty. Every day. Spring, summer, winter, fall. Weekdays or weekends. Dinner is always at five-thirty sharp.

If I'm not home by then, they'll definitely send out a search party.

I wonder if this might turn into one of those deals where everybody in town goes out into the woods and holds hands and walks in a line until somebody yells, "Chief! You gotta come look at this."

Like I said: I watch a lot of movies.

Only problem with the search party scenario? They'll have to hold hands and walk across a rocky ravine to find me. I don't think I could've picked a worse place to die.

What if nobody ever finds my body?

What if they don't even know if I'm dead and just think I'm missing, like that girl from school who disappeared like four months ago? What if I become the new Isabella Rojas?

All of a sudden, I sense that someone is watching me. Someone from above.

I look up and see a helicopter. It has WROL painted on its belly. It's the eye-in-the-sky traffic chopper from our number one local news station, off to do its rush hour traffic report.

I wave at the chopper. I know the pilot! It's Mrs. Owens. She's Christopher's mom. Yes, he's always Christopher. Never Chris. He told me Christopher is classier.

You ready for a laugh? I've been in the WROL helicopter before. Mrs. Owens took Christopher and me up for a ride once for Christopher's birthday. Some kids get piñatas or bouncy houses. We got a ride in a whirlybird.

And here's the funny part: I was terrified. The whole time.

Mrs. Owens, who was in the army for a bunch of years, tried to calm me down. While we hovered over a carpet of bumpy green treetops, she told Christopher and me that when she was serving overseas, she realized that "fear is the true enemy." She suggested that we not let fear hold us back. That we live every day as if it were our last.

Now that I've actually lived my last day, I'm not sure I would agree with Mrs. Owens's recommendation. If you live every day knowing you might die before it was over like I just did, you might never leave your house again. You might never crawl out from underneath the covers.

I'm staring straight up.

Mrs. Owens is making circles over my final resting spot. I'm pretty sure she sees me or, you know, my body.

I have to wonder: Did some supernatural force guide Mrs. Owens to the scene? Did one of my ancestors come out of that tunnel of light to guide *her* instead of me?

Her chopper floats lower. Oh, yeah. She sees me. The empty shell of me still on the rocks.

This is probably the worst day of her helicopter-piloting life.

It's time for what comes next.

I go to my own funeral.

CHAPTER 4

SOMEHOW, IN A BLINK, I'm there.

Time doesn't work the way it used to. Probably because I don't work the way I used to, either. Anyway, my four nerdy best friends are sitting together in the third row of the funeral home chapel.

By the way, in case you're thinking it, calling my friends "nerdy" isn't a bad thing. It just means we're all a little different in a middle school organized around the standard cliques. You know: the Normals, the Mean Girls, the Jocks, the Popular Squad, the Geeks, the Artistes, the Brainiacs, and the Wannabes (the kids trying hard to work their way into one of the other cliques).

My four friends and I are a strange mix of all the cliques jumbled up and poured into a weird mold nobody really recognizes. Some of us are geeky but funny; smart but never boring. One is a jock but not a jerk. We're all nerds. We don't quite fit.

Neither does the music somebody picked for my funeral. Seriously. I have never heard organ music so weepy and sad before, not even at the ice-skating rink, where I had plenty of time to focus on the organ music since my parents wouldn't let me actually skate with my friends. Sliding around the ice on thin blades instead of rubber-soled snow boots with cleats? Way too dangerous.

As the funeral music drones on, I realize this is Major Drawback #1 of dying before my time. I don't get to choose my final playlist.

Anyway, like I said, my best friends—Christopher, Annie, Axe, and Mickey—are sitting together in the third row. The first row is where my mom, my dad, and my little brother Charlie are seated. They're all so sad, which makes me feel sad, too.

Behind my family in the second row are all the relatives who could make the trip on short notice. My three living grandparents. My aunts, uncles, and cousins—including some I've only ever met once or twice at the beach for a family reunion. This one guy, cousin Rod, stole my boogie board at the reunion, which was fine by me because my dad would only let me use it in the motel's pool, not the ocean. Apparently, the ocean is full of sharks just waiting for kids like me kicking their legs behind a boogie board. You look worse than nerdy when you use a boogie board in a motel pool. You look dorky.

Some other people from school are there, too. Okay. One. The principal. I think "attending funerals for any and all dead students" is listed as a job requirement when you become principal. None of my teachers are in the chapel. Maybe because none of them know who I am or, you know, who I was. I never participated in class discussions or raised my hand to answer a question.

In that way I took my dad's advice. "Why risk it, Finn?" he'd tell me. "If you avoid all the questions, you never have to worry about giving the wrong answer. If you stay invisible, you never have to worry about looking like a fool."

Now, I guess, I really am invisible.

They have a picture of me on a placard mounted on an easel up front next to the casket. They've labeled it with my name: Finn McAllister. (Although I think most of the people in the pews already know my name.)

I can't be one hundred percent certain, but I'm pretty sure my spirit face looks the same as my eighth-grade class picture face—the one in the blown-up photo. Although I'm a little whiter, a little paler now. Very wax paper–ish.

Now I feel horrible. I see my mom. The one who insisted I buy that bright-orange bike.

She's crying.

And once she starts sobbing, so does everybody else. Including me. It's like she's given us all permission. "I'm Finn's mother and I'm crying, so you can cry, too!"

I'm so, so sorry I died. I know how much it hurt my parents. Worse than it hurt me crashing into those pointy rocks. My pain passed. My parents' pain will last for as long as they live.

Even my dad is sniffling a little (though I can tell he's trying really hard not to). That cousin who "permanently borrowed" my boogie board? Little Rod? His shoulders are shuddering. Maybe he finally regrets ripping that boogie board out of my hands at that family reunion.

The whole chapel is crying, crying, crying. According to the preacher up at the podium, I "died far too young."

I agree.

While the preacher keeps preaching, the crying becomes weeping.

Even my four friends are blubbering.

Finally, I've had enough. "All right, you guys," I say out loud, hoping somehow the people in the pews can hear me.

In fact, I'm practically screaming.

"All right, all right, all right. *STOP CRYING*. You guys? JUST STOP!!! Please?"

That's when the weirdest (but kind of amazing) thing happens.

BOOM! My friends stop crying.

Did I just make that happen?

It's like we're playing Monopoly and everybody owns Waterworks.

CHAPTER 5

OKAY. Time for a flashback.

Seeing my four best buds at my funeral isn't the best way to really get to know them. So, let's go back in time. Not too far. Just last week. My last middle school cafeteria lunch before I decided to go cruising up Ridge Rim Road on my bike.

That's right, my last meal on earth was Pizza-Filled Breadsticks. But I loved 'em. A very easy way to eat pizza without dribbling sauce and grease all over your shirt. And the smell? I don't think I ever realized how good a cafeteria-baked breadstick filled with pizza toppings like tomato sauce, meat, and cheese actually smells until now. I mean, is there a better smell on earth than fresh-baked bread of any kind? Nope. Especially when it's all warm and gooey and soaked with something like butter or pepperoni drippings. Especially when you're starving, which I was every day because we had the late lunch period.

But we didn't come back here to my final meal on earth for the food (although the chicken tenders in the deep fat fryer smell awfully good, too). So, like they say on *Family Feud*, let's meet the Lunch Bunch.

First there's me. Finn the observer. Finn the eyewitness. Finn the not-so-innocent bystander. The one who's always just a little removed from the action, watching the cool stuff everybody else is doing (because my parents won't let me do it) and then telling them, in a funny way, about what they've just done. I guess I've always been our storyteller.

And then, in Geometry, Annie told Ms. Tomlin that it was easy to find X because it was written right there on the triangle's hypotenuse.

We laughed a lot around that cafeteria table.

I'm gonna miss the laughter even more than the deep-fried food.

Next to me is Christopher. He's been my best friend since forever. He's wicked smart, which of course automatically qualifies him for nerd-dom. Ten years from now? He'll probably be a brain surgeon or a billionaire in Silicon Valley. Maybe both. I wish I could be there to see it.

Christopher (never Chris, as you recall) doesn't like to look people in the eye. So, we're all used to him staring at his shoes, his carton of milk, or whatever our T-shirts have to say that day. He's so smart, he could tell you why his mother's traffic helicopter doesn't spin around in circles when those rotary blades up top start whirling. I'm sure he could also tell you exactly what bones I broke in my tumble off Ridge Rim Road.

Next to him is Annie. She's always been kind of confusing to me. One day, she's wearing flannel shirts and jeans and splashing around in the mud to retrieve the football she heaved farther than anyone else—with a perfect spiral, by the way. The next day, she's doing girly things, like obsessing over selfies or getting into Aztec nail art.

I've kind of had an on-again, off-again crush on Annie my whole life, which I guess has to end now that, you know, my whole life is over. Duh. One time at a party we were playing Seven Minutes in Heaven and when we were in the dark closet, we talked about football. And the Vikings' chances this year. And how to throw a perfect spiral.

So, yeah. So much for seizing the romantic moment.

Did I ever end up telling her how I felt?

Are you kidding? That would've been scarier than being chased off a cliff by a maniac in a van.

Next up is Axe. Everybody thinks because he's an over-sized black kid he should be great at sports. Spoiler: He isn't. He's a terrible athlete. When we were younger and played kickball, he could strike out swinging. He'd miss the ball three times in a row—even though the pitcher was rolling it straight at his kicking foot. SWISH!

Axe is unbelievably nice to everybody. Except total jerks. (Like the ones who keep asking him why he isn't on the football team because he looks like an NFL linebacker.) Sweet as Axe is, if a jerk gets in his face (or one of his friends' faces), he will become that jerk's worst nightmare.

Finally we have Miguel or, as he likes to say, "Yo, call me Mickey. Like the baseball players, not the mouse." Mickey is an amazing athlete. Football, basketball, baseball—if it has a ball, he's on the first-string team. He's great at everything athletic, and *wow* does he know it. He's extremely cocky but he's also funny about his cockiness. "Life without me," he once told a girl, "would be like a broken pencil. Pointless."

So if Mickey is such a super jock, what's he doing sitting at the nerd table? Well, back in elementary school, when Axe's growth spurts were having growth spurts and Mickey was just Miguel and not, you know, *Mickey*, Axe used to protect him. Mickey never forgot. None of us did.

Oh, have I mentioned that girls totally love Mickey?

All of them.

Even Annie.

Anyway, let's jump back to my funeral now because I'm wondering: Did Mickey and Annie come to the chapel together? It *is* a Saturday. Was my death an excuse for them to have an early afternoon date?

I'm making my way up the center aisle to check out my friends in the third row of pews when all of a sudden, out of nowhere, I'm blinded by a light. It's beaming from behind my coffin. I see a silhouette shuffling forward.

It's my grandfather.

The one who died five years ago.

CHAPTER 6

MY GRANDFATHER on my father's side, Desmond McAllister, was very tall and skinny when he was alive.

He's still tall and skinny now that he's dead. His face is extremely stern. He always looks like he just smelled a carton of sour milk.

The last time I saw him was at my eighth birthday party. That's right. Five years ago. Way to do the math.

Not even the ice cream and cake could make him smile.

He slowly raises his hand and gestures for me to come join him in the light. "It is time," he announces in a low, spooky voice. He's giving me goose bumps. He never used to do that, back when he was alive. He was just, you know, Grandpa McAllister. The old man in the assisted living facility. I never really spent much time with him. Maybe I should've. Maybe there were a lot of things I should've done.

"We need to leave, Finnegan," he tells me. "Say your good-byes. I've come to guide you on."

Why can't my grandfather just take me fishing like other grandpas do?

I look around. Nobody in the pews can hear Grandpa McAllister. They're all crying again.

"Um, where are we going?" I ask him.

Grandpa McAllister doesn't answer. He simply turns around and starts walking back into the light. He's a slow-moving silhouette surrounded by hazy brightness. He raises his hand to point toward wherever the light is coming from. When he does, he breaks up the beam into blinding slivers.

I cover my eyes and summon my courage, something I

never really had a lot of when I was alive.

"No," I say even though my voice cracks when I say it. "I'm not going with you."

I never talked back to my grandfather like that before. I was always afraid to talk like that to scary adults. Now I figure it might be even worse because he's even scarier. He's now a ghost. A guide spirit.

He turns around to face me.

"No?" he says. *"No?!?"*

His voice echoes. Maybe it's bouncing off the walls of the light tunnel. Maybe it's some kind of special effects. Whatever it is, I'm scared.

I shake my head because I'm too petrified to speak again.

My grandfather squints at me—hard.

"Unfinished business?" he says, arching an eyebrow.

This time I nod. "Yes, sir. Uh, I have some stuff I need to take care of. Like you said, unfinished business. Business that needs finishing. . ."

I'm babbling.

Grandpa McAllister heaves a sigh and exhales a cloud of steam, like you do when you're outside playing in the snow.

"Be quick about it, Finn," he tells me. "Finish your business. Carry no regrets with you into the next life."

When he says that, his gaze drifts to the funeral crowd. Everyone is frozen in some kind of suspended animation. No one is budging. Nobody is even breathing. It looks like they're doing that viral video thing from a few years ago—the mannequin challenge.

Something glistens in my grandfather's eye. A tear? A drop of ice?

He's focused on Grandma McAllister, sitting there in the second row, dabbing her eyes with a lacy handkerchief. Frozen stiff.

She's his wife. His widow.

My grandfather swallows something that could be all the feelings he's, you know, feeling. The way he's looking at my grandmother, it makes me wonder if he had some unfinished business that he never took care of. Some regrets.

"Be quick about it, Finn," he repeats, softer this time. "Finish what needs finishing."

He turns around and heads up into the shaft of light. And then, WHOOSH! It's like someone pulled the plug on one of those giant searchlights. The tunnel of light vacuums itself down into a tiny pinpoint and disappears.

I face my funeral crowd again. People are moving. Everybody is hugging and drying their eyes and streaming out of the pews.

I'm still near the row filled with my friends.

"Come on," says Mickey, sadly. "Let's get out of here."

"Yeah," says Annie. "Let's hit the Lake."

"Sounds cool to me," adds Axe, quietly.

Christopher nods. "It's what Finn would've wanted us to do."

Christopher is correct. The Lake was probably my favorite place on the planet. Man, I loved it there.

"The Lake was probably Finn's favorite place on the planet," says Annie. "Man, he loved it there."

Okay. That's extremely freaky. Annie picked up exactly what I was thinking. Word for word. Did I, somehow, make her read my thoughts? If so, I need to watch what I think.

I'm afraid she might pick up some of my, uh, "other thoughts," too. The ones about her!

CHAPTER 7

THE LAKE'S OFFICIAL NAME is Lake Naniizaanad, which means "it is dangerous" in the indigenous Ojibwe language.

Yeah. You'd think my dad made up the name. But his family's Irish, not Native American.

Everybody just calls it "the Lake." Maybe because nobody can remember how to pronounce "Naniizaanad." The Lake, which is actually more of a swimming hole, is fed by foamy white water shooting down a steeply slanted gulley strewn with boulders. It's also rimmed by sheer cliffs, which make it great for diving—if you really, really know what you're doing and where to dive. Otherwise, as my mother and father always pointed out, you could crack open your skull. Or wind up paralyzed. Or both.

I arrive at the Lake before my friends. They'll probably be riding their bikes. Me? I thought about being here and—WHOOSH!—now I am. Transportation seems to be super easy when you don't have a body to haul around.

The Lake has always been a special place for me and my friends. It's where we went every day in the summer, if we could. It's where I first saw a girl in a two-piece bathing suit. It's also where Annie slugged me in the shoulder while I stared at the first girl I'd ever seen in a two-piece bathing suit.

The Lake is where I always had a great time watching my friends having a great time. I'd watch all the cool stuff they did and then tell them stories about how cool it was. I was kind of our historian.

Diving is strictly prohibited. Especially in my family.

Before long, I hear my four friends pumping their mountain bikes up the steep trail to the top of the cliffs. The jumping rocks. Mickey is in the lead, of course. Axe brings up the rear. They're all huffing and puffing. I'm the only one not breathing hard. In fact, I'm not breathing at all.

"That felt great," says Mickey when he reaches the top, half a minute before everybody else. "Gave my quads an awesome workout."

"Exercise has been proven to help people process grief," says Christopher between pants for breath as he pulls into the lookout point.

"I'm just glad to be out of that funeral home," says Annie.

Axe nods. "Everything was so sad," he says gently.

"Uh, hello?" says Annie. "Earth to Axe. It was a funeral. What were you expecting?"

Axe shrugs. "I don't know. Maybe some funny stories about Finn?"

"Yeah," says Mickey. "There's a ton of those."

Christopher nods. "Funny stories would've been way better than organ music."

"Finn would've hated that organ music," adds Axe.

I did! I did! It was worse than the old guy on the pipe organ at the ice rink, I try to tell them. It feels just like old times. We're all up on the diving rocks. Shooting the bull. Having fun.

The only problem?

I'm still dead. They can't hear me.

"Hey," says Annie, "remember that time when I caught Finn gawking at that high school girl up here? The one in the string bikini?"

"Yeah," says Mickey, puffing up his chest. "Her top came off when she dove in. I had to dive in and rescue it for her."

"Such a gentleman," cracks Annie. "Finn almost jumped in to lend you a hand. *Almost.*"

"I don't think he ever even cannonballed off the cliff," says Axe.

"When *you* do," Annie says, "you drain half the Lake."

"Hey, it always refills itself."

"Finn's parents told him that jumping in the Lake was too dangerous," says Christopher. "Even if you did it feet first." He points down at the water. "Even if you did it right here, over the deep spot where no one has ever touched the bottom."

"Remember how he'd hurry down and meet us on the shoreline?" says Mickey. "And he'd do it sooooo carefully. Holding on to rocks. Making sure he had 'three points of contact at all times.'"

Then he starts imitating me, even though I don't think my voice ever really sounded like I'd been sucking helium out of a balloon.

"I'll race you down to the water, guys. Bet I beat you!" That was his corny line all the time. *Bet I beat you.*

"Sometimes," says Axe, "I'd wait until Finn made it all the

way down to the shore. He'd sit, right on that smooth rock down there. And then I'd leap off the ledge, tuck in my legs, turn myself into a ginormous cannonball, and splatter Finn with one of those half-of-the-lake splash landings Annie was talking about."

My friends all laugh. I can tell: they really do miss me.

"Well," says Mickey, shedding his shirt and shorts to reveal his bathing suit. "Here's to Finn. This dive is for you, buddy!"

Christopher, Axe, and Annie all strip down to their bathing suits, too.

"For Finn!" says Axe, inching closer to the ledge. "Sure, he was a chicken, but he was *our* chicken!"

"Bruck, bruck, bruck," cackles Mickey. Pretty soon they all join in the chicken squawk chorus. I don't mind. In fact, I kind of enjoy it. Reminds me of old times. Good times.

My friends move forward to the lip of the cliff. Their toes are already twiddling over the ledge, eager to jump.

"CAREFUL, YOU GUYS!" I shout from my safe spot several feet behind them. "ANNIE? WATCH IT. YOU COULD SLIP AND FALL. NO DIVING! JUST JUMP! AXE? DO A CANNONBALL! YOU, TOO, CHRISTOPHER! HELLO? ARE YOU GUYS LISTENING TO ME?"

They all turn around and actually look my way.

Did they freakin' hear me?

For a split second, all four of their faces have slightly curious expressions. It's like that chirping bird all over again.

But, just as quickly, they spin around to face the Lake again.

"Here's to Finn!" shouts Annie as she jumps off the cliff, feetfirst.

"Finn!" shout Axe, Mickey, and Christopher.

They all leap off the rocks.

Except Mickey, of course. He jumps in, headfirst, and executes a perfect, Olympics-style dive.

Because of course he does.

CHAPTER 8

MY FRIENDS DON'T LINGER long at the Lake.

In fact, they just do that one jump (or, in Mickey's case, one extremely dangerous swan dive), climb back up to the top of the rocks, grab their clothes, and, after a very emotional (if soggy and squishy) group hug, hop on their bikes to pedal home.

They're all super sad. Me, too. And not just because I'm, you know, dead. I feel bad that I'm the one who's made them all feel so bad. Of course, it isn't totally my fault. There was that drive-a-kid-off-a-cliff-and-run driver. The speed demon in the van. The maniac who was gunning up the hill behind me.

But nobody knows about him. Or her. Like I said, I didn't get a very good look at the driver. I was sort of busy, especially after I did a double somersault off Ridge Rim Road.

I decide to follow Christopher home. Actually, it's less of a decision, more of a reflex. It's what I'd always do after we hit the Lake.

When the gang rumbled down the bike trail on their rides, I closed my eyes and, when I opened them—WHOOSH!

I'm standing in the Owenses' driveway, where I've stood a billion times, ever since I was five or six and would yell, "Can Christopher come out and play today?" I see stuff I probably saw a billion times before as if I'm seeing it for the first time. Like how the basketball goal over the garage is just a hoop. The net has been missing ever since Christopher and I took over this asphalt court from his big brothers. We never thought about replacing it.

I'm still not sure how all this ghost stuff works but, I have to say, so far getting from Point A to Point B is super easy. Also, it turns out, I can walk through doors. That's right. I can walk straight through the solid wood front door and step into Christopher's house.

I'm expecting—no, I'm *hoping*—to see the typical chaos of the Owens household. Christopher has four brothers: Tom, Jeff, Steve, and Bill. Yep. His mom had five boys in seven years. They're their own basketball team, which they sometimes play indoors, especially on rainy days. They use a pair of wastepaper baskets on either side of the house—one in the den, one in the living room—as buckets. They also use a regulation Spalding for their indoor dunks. It's fun. It's also total chaos.

Mr. and Mrs. Owens (the traffic helicopter pilot) let their kids run wild and tear around the house. As long as they do well in school, they can play all they want at home. Their parenting style seems to work. Like I said, Christopher, who's the middle son, is a whiz. Smartest kid at my school. His older brothers are the smartest kids at the high school. His two younger siblings? One is the world's smartest sixth grader, and the other is tearing up academic records at the elementary school.

Sometimes, when I was hanging out at Christopher's house, I wanted to invite my parents to come witness the chaos. "See? They're running wild. They're having fun. They're laughing their heads off. Nobody's getting hurt. And, they're all bringing home straight-A's!"

But I never actually did that. Instead I kept Christopher's house as my escape. A place where, for just a few hours, I didn't have to worry about all the things my mom and dad wanted me to worry about.

But after my funeral, nobody is running around the Owens house. They're all in the den, slowly sliding their Monopoly pieces around the game board. Whoa. Usually, when the Owenses play Monopoly, it's as frantic as one of their indoor basketball scrimmages. If you buy a hotel and Tom or Jeff is the banker, they'll fling it at you. Hard. Bill tries to palm your orange five-hundred-dollar bills when you're busy rolling the dice. Steve is famous for tipping the board over if he's nearing bankruptcy. Monopoly is, usually, a full contact sport at the Owens house.

They all look so sad. Maybe everybody pulled a
GO DIRECTLY TO JAIL card.

Not today.

They're all sitting silently around their dad's faded green-felt poker table. Mrs. and Mr. Owens are in their recliners, staring blankly at the TV screen, which, by the way, is also blank. The energy has been sapped out of the room. Their house. Their lives.

By me.

Finally, Bill, the youngest, pipes up.

"Hey, Mom? Remember that time you took Christopher and Finn up in your helicopter?"

She smiles a little. Then she laughs.

"It was Christopher's tenth birthday," she remembers. "Finn didn't want me to lift off. He asked me if we could stay parked on the helipad with the blades running."

"He wanted it to be like that kiddie ride in front of the supermarket," says Tom, who apparently has heard this story before.

"He kept looking around for the quarter slot," jokes Christopher.

"Or the Off button," cracks Jeff.

It's true. I did all that. I also asked a lot of questions about gravity.

"And then, when we were up in the air?" says Mrs. Owens.

"Finn's face was greener than the treetops!" shouts Steve.

I have a queasy feeling that everybody in the Owens house knows about that birthday flight we took when Christopher turned ten. I'm legendary. A funny family story for someone else's family.

"He didn't puke, though," says Christopher with a big smile. "However, he also didn't eat any pizza when we got to Chuck E. Cheese! He asked the big mouse at the front door if he had any nausea medicine for kids."

The whole family is laughing.

Me, too.

It's funny. I wish I could go back and get airsick again, especially if it would make everybody in my "second family" smile and laugh. I feel horrible about what I've done to the Owens by dying like that.

I feel even worse about what I've done to my own family.

Yeah. I definitely have some unfinished business to take care of.

I can't put it off any longer.

I need to go visit Mom, Dad, and Charlie. I need to go home.

CHAPTER 9

AND SO I HEAD to my house.

But I don't "jump cut" or WHOOSH! my way there.

I walk. I figure it might be the last time I ever walk these three blocks from Christopher's house to mine, a walk I've taken a million times. I also need to think.

I've been doing that a lot ever since I died.

Did I live a good life? Did I make a difference in the world? Will my mother and father ever forgive me? Will Charlie be okay without a big brother? Maybe Axe can protect him, too.

Going home was going to be super tricky. My parents would be so disappointed in me. Not only did I go and die, I went and did it in what I'm sure they thought was a very dumb way.

It's nearly summer. Flowers are in bloom in all the yards. I never really smelled them before. They smell great. Yes, I'm actually taking time to stop and smell the roses. Something I probably should've done every time I walked these sidewalks but I was always in a hurry to get to Christopher's or get home in time for that five-thirty dinner bell.

So much rushing. Now? I have an eternity to miss all the stuff I skipped when I was alive.

I stand on our front porch for what seems like hours, afraid to walk through my own front door. I think about going back to Christopher's house. Then I stall some more by walking through the big oak tree in our front yard, the one Mom and Dad never let me climb, because I could fall and hurt myself, which, ta-dah, is exactly what I did up on Ridge Rim Road. I fell. I hurt myself. They were right. It ends badly.

But I want to see if I can walk through something solid besides a door. I can. Next up? Maybe a car? Can I let a car drive straight through me? How about a van? Maybe I should've been dead before I had my run-in with the van on Ridge Rim Road. I might still be alive.

Okay. That makes no sense. It's time to quit stalling.

I go back to the porch and stare at my front door some more.

Is this still my house? I wonder. I mean, I don't actually "live" there anymore. You have to be alive to do that.

I guess I should've asked Grandpa McAllister for some deets about my new home—wherever he wanted to take me. What's it like at the far end of that tunnel? Also, do they turn off that blazing light at night so people can sleep? Speaking of sleep, do you even need to do that after you are dead?

So many questions. They keep me on the porch for at least another fifteen minutes.

Well, that's what I think. Time is all warped. What feels like ten or fifteen minutes to me could be just a few seconds in the land of the living. It could be a few days.

I can't stall any longer.

I have to confront my worst fears.

That's extremely hard for me to do because all those years of leading a risk-averse, danger-avoiding life haven't done much to increase my courage quotient. I have very little experience on the fear-confronting front. My friends are right. I'm still a chicken.

A big fat dead chicken.

Bruck, bruck, bruckity bruck.

CHAPTER 10

* * * * * * * * * * *

FINALLY, I STEP THROUGH THE DOOR and enter what had, for thirteen years, been my home.

The foyer is connected on one side to the living room. Go ahead. Chuckle. Yes, smarty, I'm the dead kid in the *living* room.

I'm remembering all those Christmas mornings past. Our tree was always set up in the living room, right in front of the big bay window looking out over the street. It was an artificial tree, of course, like I said before. With LED-only lights. The kind that never heated up. Real trees decorated with old-school colored bulbs are fire hazards. So are too many extension cords. And space heaters and all sorts of wintery stuff.

I'm going to miss Christmas. I'll even miss that pine-scented room freshener Mom always hid behind the tree.

I don't need to glance at a clock to know it's five-thirty.

Mom, Dad, and my little brother, Charlie, are just sitting down to dinner in the dining room, which is just off the living room. It smells like macaroni and cheese. Some kind of casserole we've never had before. I guess neighbors and friends have been bringing meals. That's nice. People do a lot of good stuff and most of it, to be honest, I never even noticed.

"Would you care for a roll?" Mom asks Dad.

"No, thank you."

"May I please have the salt?" asks Charlie.

"Use it sparingly," says Dad, handing my little brother the tiny silver shaker. "Too much salt can give you high blood pressure."

"It will also make you retain water," adds Mom.

Okay. I know what you're thinking. *Dude. Your parents are sooooo un-chill. If they were wound any tighter, they'd be braids.*

To which I reply: *Hey, cut them some slack. Their oldest son just died.*

My parents aren't bad people. They're cautious people.

They're all still dressed in their funeral clothes. Guess it's still Saturday.

"We forgot to say grace," announces Mom, putting down her silverware.

They reach out and hold each other's hands, making a family circle around the dinner table. I realize that the family circle is a lot harder to pull off without me in my usual seat to Mom's right, Dad's left. The circle has a hole in it.

Their leaning across my empty place makes Mom start crying again.

"Poor Finn," she says softly.

Charlie starts sniffling. "I miss him, too."

Dad pushes back from the table. Folds his napkin, very tidily, and places it in his lap. Finally, he sits up straight in his chair. When he's all set, when he has a firm grip on all his emotions, he speaks: "This shouldn't have happened!"

I miss being with you guys even more than you're missing me.

CHAPTER 11

DAD DOESN'T STOP THERE.

"He should've been more careful. I always told Finn to be careful."

Mom nods. Sadly. "Yes, dear. You did."

"Of course, nobody ever listens to me. I'm sorry. But I know my numbers. It's my job to know how risky life can be."

My father works for a major insurance company. He's what they call an "actuary." His job? Using statistics to figure out when people, on average, will die, or wreck their car, or have their houses burn down. And then, he uses statistical magic to estimate the financial impact of all those tragedies.

"He shouldn't've died so young," Dad continues. "Yes, children and adolescents have the highest rate of bicycle-related injuries—approximately one-third. But they don't die. Death by bicycle is more common among adults aged fifty to fifty-nine."

This is how Dad deals with his emotions. He buries them

under a mountain of facts and numbers. He knows a lot of statistics. One for just about everything. For instance, did you know that fishing is the most dangerous occupation in the United States? Check out the numbers that Dad shared with us one night when we were eating fish sticks: The fatal injury rate for fishing workers is way higher than the fatal injury rate for truck drivers, roofers, electric line installers, or even coal miners.

Dad's shoulders slump. Tears well up in his eyes.

My friends might use humor to deal with their grief but Dad's been trying to use statistics. And I sense that his stony wall of numbers just came tumbling down.

"I miss him," he says, his voice breaking. "I miss Finn. My boy. My son."

Dad is crying. He buries his face in his hands and weeps.

Charlie looks frightened. Our father doesn't cry. He usually lets Mom do it for him. Now he can't stop sobbing. After a moment, Mom and Charlie start crying, too.

Seeing your little brother with tears streaming down his cheeks, tears you put there? Worst feeling in the world.

I can't stand to watch this any longer. It's too sad. So, so sad.

I turn away from the dinner table and fix my gaze on a framed photo we have of Grandpa McAllister. It's hanging on a dining room wall filled with other framed family photos. Some are antiques. Faded and brownish. The faces staring back at me are all Irish. Our ancestors. The McAllister and

O'Keefe clans (my mom was an O'Keefe). I don't really know who half the faces are but I figure I'll be meeting them all soon enough.

Suddenly, the portrait of Grandpa McAllister starts to move.

CHAPTER 12

"ARE YOU READY TO MOVE ON, Finnegan?" Grandpa McAllister asks me from inside his picture frame. "Have you finished your unfinished business?"

I panic. The living portrait of a dead ancestor is freaking me out.

"Maybe," I say. "I mean, no actually. Not really. There's still stuff I need to do. Stuff I probably should've done a long time ago."

Grandpa McAllister steps out of the wall and looks down at my family—his son, daughter-in-law, and only living grandson, Charlie. They're all sobbing, stricken with grief. Hurting because I hurt them.

"Haven't you done enough?" he asks.

I summon up enough courage to attempt a question. "Grandpa?"

"What?"

This is worse than the haunted mansion at Disney World!

"Why is my dad the way he is? Why is he so nervous? So afraid of life?"

"Your father has his reasons," is all Grandpa will say.

He summons me with his bony hand. The wall behind him dissolves into a tunnel filled with light. "It is time for you to leave here," he tells me. "Come along."

He turns his back on me and starts leading the way into the tunnel.

I realize I have a major decision to make.

I can go with Grandpa and meet all the dead ancestors from our dining room wall. I can, like the funeral preacher said, move on to my heavenly reward, whatever that reward might be.

Or, I can haunt my friends and family as an invisible ghost until I'm really ready to move on. Until I finish whatever unfinished business I feel gluing me to the life I know I have to leave behind.

Suddenly, Dad slams both his fists down on the table. Silverware jangles. Ice cubes rattle in water glasses.

"Why did Finn have to be so stupid? Why'd he have to pull such a foolish stunt? Trying to jump his bike over a stone wall on a cliff like he was some kind of X-sports daredevil in a video game? What was he thinking?"

Whoa, I think. *I'll tell you what I'm thinking right now: That's not what happened, Dad! Not at all!*

Of course I'm the only one who knows that.

That's when it hits me.

I have to investigate my own death. I need to find my killer. Because I need to somehow show my father, not to mention the whole world, that my death wasn't caused by me being stupid.

A speed demon maniac in a Stephen King van chased me off Ridge Rim Road!

And I'm going to prove it.

I have no idea *how* I'm going to prove it, but I will, even if it's the last thing I ever do.

Which, duh, I guess it will be.

"Sorry, Grandpa," I shout at his back as he moves farther

49

and farther away. "I'm not coming with you. I need to stay here. I need to find my killer!"

Grandpa keeps on walking.

The light disappears.

I'm on my own.

CHAPTER 13

I LEAVE THE HOUSE and head to...

The Ice Cream Shoppe.

Not exactly sure how or why that happened but here I am. The place is closed. The glowing clock behind the counter tells me it's three o'clock. In the morning. The streets outside are dark and deserted.

It's just me and the ice cream. Forty-five different flavors. More if you include the fruity sherbet, but come on, who really does?

When I was alive, the only ice cream I ever ate was vanilla. Or chocolate chip. I never ventured very far down the flavor menu board. But now, I see all those open tubs in the freezer case. All those bright colors and fun swirls of nuts and chocolate and marshmallows and candy bits.

I know I should be searching for my killer, but I want to live a little and taste all the ice cream flavors.

And so I do. Mostly because I figure that if I take one little

Now this is living! Maybe I should've done it while I was actually alive.

pink plastic sample spoon bite out of all the open cardboard barrels lined up behind the glass, no one will ever notice that anything is missing. They won't call the exterminators or the Ghostbusters. They might if I gobbled up my usual two scoops of vanilla, though.

I work my way down the line and sample strawberry, chocolate, coffee, Oreo, mango, coconut, matcha, and even avocado. Then I try the even wilder flavors. Chocolate coconut almond chocolate chip. Black raspberry double chocolate brownie. Cookie dough. Cotton candy. Ice cream with peanut butter cups, candy cane chunks, and breakfast cereal in it. And, yes, I even taste the raspberry sorbet.

It's all so good!

Using the small pink spoons turns out to be an excellent plan. There's very little evidence that I was ever here.

And I realize, this is the kind of smart thinking I need to start doing to clear my name. To show my dad, and the whole world, that I didn't die because I did something stupid with my bike. I need to start being more analytical like my father. Not all the way to statistics-graphing-calculator-clipped-to-my-belt analytical. Just more logical. I need to Sherlock Holmes my way toward finding my killer and finishing my unfinished business.

For instance, who was driving the black van that ran me off the road? Did they leave skid marks or tire tracks? This is when I wish I had paid more attention to all those CSI TV shows.

And I have to ask myself this horrible question, the one they always ask in murder mysteries: Did I have any. . .enemies?

To be honest, thinking about who might've wanted me dead isn't much fun. In fact, it's downright depressing. I never did anything to get myself an enemy. I never did anything at all.

I need to chill. That means I need to kick back and play some video games.

BOOM.

I'm in my front yard again.

I look up at my second story bedroom window. I wonder if my game gear is still where I left it. Or did Mom and Dad, in a fit of rage at my MXGP Pro Enduro motocross biking game, chuck my PS4 into the trash?

I float up for a closer look.

Yup, you read that right: float. Don't ask me how I did it. I just did.

Anyway, the floating part is awesome. The view through my bedroom window?

It kind of sucks.

CHAPTER 14

SURE, MY PS4 is still exactly where I left it. But so is everything else in my room. My socks are still balled up on the floor near my dirty underwear for the week. My kicks are in a heap in front of the closet door. My posters and books and lamps and piles of game boxes are all still exactly where they were when I left home to go to school on June sixth.

My room is quickly becoming a Jurassic Park mosquito frozen inside a chunk of amber. Or a room in a house where a famous dead person used to live. Will Mom and Dad string a red velvet rope across the doorway and let people stand in the hallway to gaze at all my stuff? To study the junk heap of my life that I left behind? If so, I really wish I had picked up all that dirty laundry.

My bedroom, my whole house, is just so sad. I remember my classic line that I'd use when one of my friends looked all bummed out and I was trying to cheer them up: "What? Did somebody die?"

Uh, yeah. This time they did. And it was me.

Knowing my own home is not going to be such a fun place to hang around, I zoom over to Christopher's house. I am not going there to haunt the guy, though. (Unless my unfinished business isn't finished before Halloween; spooking my friends on Halloween would be awesome and I'd definitely have the best costume—even if nobody could see it.)

I just need to go to my home away from home and forget about being dead for a while.

It's now four in the morning, according to the grandfather clock in Christopher's living room that I just walked through. I don't want to wake up Christopher or his brothers or his parents. I'm not sure if I could, actually. I still haven't made much noise that anybody can hear. Just a few weird connections that could've been coincidences. To be safe, I head downstairs to their family room. That's where the TV and video games are.

I spend a few hours watching Netflix. And Disney Plus. And Apple TV. And Hulu. And Amazon Prime. Christopher's family subscribes to more streaming services than most rivers. At my house we have basic cable.

And since the dead never sleep, I can do a major binge-marathon.

After my second movie, I start hearing footsteps and a coffee maker gurgling. The Owens family is waking up. I'll

Wow! I finally have enough time to watch all the Star Wars movies, shows, and cartoons!

have to wait to play video games or complete my Obi-Wan Kenobi marathon.

I carefully creep up the stairs. Fortunately, I don't squeak any boards as I climb the steps. Yes, I could just float or transport myself into the Owenses' kitchen but, somehow, it feels good to walk. To remember how excited everybody gets when a baby takes its first step. A few months after that magical moment, most of us take walking for granted. It's really a miracle when you think about it, and, like I said, I've been doing a lot of thinking lately.

I reach the top of the staircase and smell bacon.

And coffee.

And, best of all, pancakes!

It's Sunday morning at Christopher's house!

CHAPTER 15

I HOVER IN THE DINING ROOM with Christopher, his mom, and his brothers as their dad makes pancakes for everybody in the kitchen.

It smells delicious.

All that bubbly batter, sizzling bacon, hot maple syrup, and melting butter. I'm trying not to drool, the way I did that time I spent the night at Christopher's and had a stack of his dad's flapjacks the next morning.

If I drool, I'm afraid Mr. Owens may see a puddle on the floor and think his roof just sprung a leak. Would my ghosty drool dribble real liquid? I don't know and I don't want to find out.

The Owens boys pass around the squeeze bottle of syrup. By the time it gets to Billy, the youngest, its sides are so sticky the bottle is glued to Billy's hands. Until Steve tugs it away. The bottle makes a rude sound.

"Did your hands just fart?" jokes Tom, the oldest.

The Owenses all laugh. Including Mr. and Mrs. Owens. For some reason, that makes me sad. I guess it's because my dad would never laugh at a fart joke. He'd just frown and scowl and make you wish you could crawl under the table and disappear.

Mrs. Owens flaps open the Sunday paper.

"Maybe we should go to the movies today," she suggests. "A movie might cheer us all up."

She suggests a romantic comedy. Mr. Owens wants to see a spy thriller. Each of the boys wants to see something different. That's when I realize: I can see them all! I just have to walk through the walls separating the theaters inside the multiplex!

Another dead guy bonus? Unlimited free movie passes.

The multiplex at the mall has sixteen screens!

I'm tempted to snag a slice of bacon and a bite of pancake before I go but that would probably freak my friends out. Floating bacon and tiny triangles of pancake tend to do that. Besides, I had all that ice cream. And there's popcorn at the movies!

The theater isn't too crowded first thing Sunday morning. But movies do start at eleven. So I walk through the sliding glass doors that used to automatically glide open but now don't because they can't see me. Nobody wants to tear my ticket. Because the staff can't see me, either. At least the lobby smells like it always has. You know—popcorn kernels crushed into the carpet.

I walk through the door to theater one. I figure I'll work my way up from one to sixteen. Until I do the math and realize that would probably take thirty-two hours, which is fine by me, because I don't need to sleep. But the folks running the digital projectors? They'd probably like to go home from time to time and hang out with their families, maybe watch a movie.

So, I'm going to be picky.

The first theater I enter is showing an R-rated film. Chalk up another victory for the dead because I'm only thirteen. I'm not supposed to see this movie without a parent or guardian for four more years. My father would hate this flick. It has all sorts of risky stunts. Motorcycles leaping across rooftops. People dangling out of helicopters. Explosions.

In fact, it's making me kind of queasy. Maybe it's just a little too soon. One wreck in particular reminds me of my own.

I decide to leave the scary film before the big finale and slide through the wall to whatever is next door.

Singing animals. Nice computer animation. Several celebs singing the songs. I'm pretty sure the woodchuck is that girl who won all the Grammy Awards. To make sure, I stick around and watch the beginning. Oh, yeah. It's her. I see her name right there in the opening credits.

Whoa! Use your turn signal next time, buddy. Your car insurance rates are gonna shoot through the roof!

Next, I slide through the other wall and check out a cheesy comedy. It's stupid. Stupid *good*. Lots of laughs.

I recognize one of those laughs, and not just because it's the loudest in the darkened room.

It's my friend Mickey!

CHAPTER 16

IT LOOKS LIKE MICKEY is on a Sunday date with Abby, one of the cheerleaders who loves watching Mickey score touchdowns or nail three-pointers.

They're both yukking it up.

Casually, Mickey fakes a yawn and extends his arm so it ends up on Abby's shoulder. All of a sudden, he's basically hugging her. What can I say? The guy has smooth moves—on and off the field.

I could never be like Mickey. I'd be too afraid. I'd probably do the yawn thing with my Coke hand and dump ice down the girl's back.

But I wish I had the chance to try. Not right away. Maybe when I was in high school.

I'm going to miss high school. Completely.

"Thanks for coming with me," Mickey whispers in Abby's ear. Yes. I'm hovering right behind them over an empty seat that still looks empty to them because I'm invisible. "I needed a few laughs. . .after. . .you know. . .yesterday. . .the funeral."

Mickey looks like he's all choked up.

Abby says, "Everything will be okay."

Then—she kisses him. There are wet, slurping noises. Gross. These guys were just sharing a big bucket of buttered popcorn.

I've seen enough.

I need to move on to the next movie.

Like I said, I can stay at the movie theater as late as I want to. Yes, it's a school night but I don't have to go to school on Monday morning! I'm on permanent summer, fall, winter, *and* spring break.

The multiplex stops showing movies around midnight. And it isn't that exciting watching workers sweep up popcorn, collect crumpled Coke cups, and scrape up Junior Mints glued to the floor.

But when you don't have to wake up for anything the next morning, when you don't even need to sleep, the night is always young.

This calls for a video game! I can play them all night if I want to!

So after my twelve-hour, six-movie marathon (okay, I watched the kiddie cartoon thing three times in total), I decide to head home.

To my house.

I'm afraid if I go to Christopher's house too often, I'll end up as a poltergeist there. Like in that other movie. Poltergeists get glued to a certain spot and spook it for all time. I don't want to end up trapped inside Christopher's walls or attic where I'd have to spend my nights making loud noises.

So I jump cut home and float up to my room. Nothing's been touched, same as before.

I fire up my PS4 and play that motocross biking game I know my parents must hate. It's fun. For about five minutes. Then all the jumps and stunts start reminding me of the jump and stunt that didn't work out so well up on Ridge Rim Road. I'm thinking, in the future, I'll stick to nonthreatening video games. The ones where all you have to do is pop candy or run a diner or whatever.

Suddenly, my bedroom door creaks open.

It's my dad!

CHAPTER 17

"FINN?"

He sounds spooked. He looks at the video game console. It's on. Glowing. A stunt bike frozen in mid-leap. I can hear its soundtrack, which is very DUN-DUN-ish and action packed. Dad heard it, too, I bet. In fact, my whining motocross stunt bike's sound effects are probably what woke him up at one o'clock in the morning.

Ooops. At Christopher's house, the TV was way down in the basement. Nobody could hear all the noise (lots of explosions and *Star Wars* orchestra music). Here at my house, I'm two doors down from my parents' bedroom.

I take a few steps backward, pass through my desk, and try to hide behind it. Dad is staring right at me. It feels as if he can see through me, which maybe he can if he sees me at all.

Dad frowns and lunges forward. His fingers are out and ready to throttle me for dying so stupidly.

At least that's what I think is going on until he rips my

Now I wish I was even more invisible!

PS4 console off my desk, disconnecting all the cords with a yank so hard it swivels the monitor.

"Stupid game," he mutters. "You killed Finn!"

Dad stomps out of my bedroom with my very expensive, biggest-Christmas-gift-of-all-time PS4 tucked under his arm. I think he's taking it down to the garage to toss it into a recycling bin. Right after he smashes it to plastic bits with a sledgehammer.

I find it kind of odd that Dad didn't puzzle over what turned the game on. He probably thinks these machines are just automatically on all the time in their evil, never-ending quest to entice kids into doing reckless stuff.

Like performing death-defying stunts on their bicycles.

CHAPTER 18

SO NOW I KNOW I can't play loud video games or watch action-packed movies without muting the sound.

Or maybe putting on headphones or popping in my earbuds. But I'm not sure they would work.

So there's not much to do early Monday morning. I wish the sun would hurry up and rise and, *BOOM!* It does.

I don't think I made the sun rise.

It's been doing that all by itself since the dawn of time. I think I am now able to fast-forward on the timeline that crawls so slowly for most eighth graders. We're always in a hurry to grow up, never thinking about what comes after you do that. Now that I've already reached the final stop in the game of life, I wish I could've slowed things down. Not been in such a hurry to grow up and grow old.

Having gloomy-goosed my way into becoming a total saddo, I decide to head to school even though I don't have to. I guess it's just a bad habit. What else would I do at seven on a Monday morning? Plus, I wouldn't mind hanging out with my besties a little longer. Maybe one of them has heard something about the van driver. I realize that while I was off at the movies and playing video games, I was supposed to be solving my own murder.

Yeah. It's a focus thing. All my report cards said I have "concentration issues." Guess those teachers were right. I wish I had paid more attention to what they were trying to teach me because no one is going to try to teach me it again.

I jump cut out of my bedroom without, for the first time ever, worrying about how my hair looks or what to wear to school. I drift up the sidewalk a couple doors to Annie's house. She and I have walked to school together since first grade. She comes out, looking beautiful, just like she always did. But today she also looks sad. Her head is hanging low. Her shoulders sag.

I remember she can't see me. In her world, she is walking to school without me for the very first time. She looks up the block to my house, as if she thinks I'm just a little late, that I'll come running out my front door munching on a Pop-Tart saying, "sorry, sorry, sorry," which is what I said every time I was late.

She sighs and wipes away a tear.

"Finn's gone, Annie," I hear her tell herself. She sounds a little like a coach trying to buck up her team at halftime. "He's never coming back. Okay? He's gone. Dead. Deal with it, girl."

Well, this definitely stinks. I've turned Annie into a saddo, too.

Whoa, I think. *She's being a little hard on herself.*

I put my arm around Annie. Not that I'm trying to match Mickey's moves at the movie theater, but I figure she needs a hug.

She shivers the instant my arm drapes over her shoulders. Her teeth even chatter.

Did I do that? Can Annie feel that I'm here?

I didn't mean to spook her or give her goose bumps. I guess I'm not totally in control of everything as a ghost.

Huh. In some ways, being dead is just like being alive.

CHAPTER 19

SOME THINGS IN LIFE never change—even after you die.

Annie is strolling along, her head down, earbuds in, hands jammed inside her hoodie pockets. I know Annie. This is what I call her sad/mad walk. She's still thinking about me. Which is sweet but also bitter. Guess that's why they invented that word *bittersweet*. It's not just for chocolate.

Here comes the part that never changes.

Annie reaches the end of our block and hangs a right.

The Dussendorf brothers, Frank and Joe, are waiting for her. Like always, their arms are crossed over their chests. Like always, they block the sidewalk. Like always, they act like total jerks.

"Aw, why are you so sad, Annie Fanny?" Frank says with a baby talk voice.

Annie tilts up her head so she can give him her laser-focused stink eye.

"Why are you such a jerk, Frank?"

Yes, I know I'm the ghost, but these two guys are scaring me!

"Ooooh," says Joe, who's older and in high school. "She's right. We're not allowed to make fun of girls' butts anymore. It's against the rules. The rules suck, but they're the rules."

"Fine," says Frank. "Why are you so sad, Annie Bananie? Is it because your boyfriend took a header off a cliff, cracked open his skull, and died?"

"Too bad about that," sneers Joe. "But I have to wonder: Was Finn McAllister just stupid or was he scared? He was always such a chicken whenever we bumped into you two."

It's true. The Dussendorf brothers always terrified me. Annie was much braver. When they tried to torment us, she usually cracked some kind of joke that made them laugh long enough that they forgot about killing us.

Wait a second. . .

Joe Dussendorf is in high school. He's over sixteen! He probably has a driver's license. His family might even own a black van. Did our local neighborhood bullies pull the biggest school bully stunt in recorded history? Did these two madmen run me off the road? I mean it's definitely a possibility. They are right on the edge of juvenile delinquent–dangerous.

Today, Annie doesn't seem to have a snappy comeback for the Dussendorfs. Maybe because she's just too bummed out to crack a joke.

So she decides to make a run for it.

She dashes out into the street and sprints up the road.

"Hey!" shouts Frank, racing after her. "You forgot to pay the toll!"

"You have to give us something good from your lunch!" adds Joe, joining in the chase.

I can zip along faster than any of them. I literally fly up the street until I'm halfway between Annie and the two thugs in hot pursuit. I land, spin around, put up both my arms and yell, "Stop! Leave Annie alone!"

The brothers don't hear me. They don't see me.

In fact, Frank—the meaty, sweaty one—runs right through me. Yes, it's disgusting. Frank Dussendorf slithering through my ghostly form feels like slime oozing between my fingers.

But he shivers. The way people do when they walk through a spiderweb they didn't see coming. And the chills slow him down some. There's nothing more I can do. Annie is on her own.

Fortunately, she's fast. She could star on the cross country team if she didn't find all that "jock stuff" boring. But, as she nears the crosswalk closest to the middle school, she slows down.

The Dussendorf brothers don't.

Until they see Axe.

Yep. Axe, our gentle giant friend, is also on the school crossing guard squad. They had to stitch together a custom reflective sash for him because his chest is so wide.

"Morning, Annie," says Axe. "How you doing?"

"Better," she says with a smile. "Now."

Axe glares at Frank and Joe.

He doesn't say anything. He doesn't have to. Everyone knows how much he hates jerks. The Dussendorfs? Maximum jerkitude and jerkosity.

"Um, have a good day at school, Frankie," says Joe, his voice quivering. He's pretending he's just another high schooler dutifully escorting his little brother to middle school.

Then he takes off running.

CHAPTER 20

SO NOW I HAVE my first suspect.

Joe "Jerk Face" Dussendorf. I definitely need to check out what kind of vehicles the Dussendorf family has parked in their driveway. If there's a black van, then I'll know I have my man. Maybe. I mean there *are* a ton of black vans on the road.

Anyhow, it'd be a start.

But I'm not doing it now because, okay, I'm a little distracted. Being back at middle school when you're a ghost? It's awesome. And not just because you can walk through steel doors and see what everybody has stashed in their lockers. (Some of you do way too much interior decorating.)

I can hang around with my friends. I can hang around with other people, too—all those cliques I never belonged to. It's a great way to pick up ALL the gossip. I mean every shred. No one can see me so they don't stop talking when I sneak up behind them. Before the second bell rings, I know more about who has a crush on who than I ever have.

I also hear a lot about me.

"It's so sad. Was his name really Finn? Like in Huckleberry?"

"I never really knew the guy."

"He was in my English class. I think."

"Why'd he do something so dumb?"

"They should close down Ridge Rim Road. It's too dangerous."

I decide to stick with my usual schedule. I know, I know. I should go to classes I've never gone to before. Learn things I've never even thought about learning before. But remember, I'm still, basically, Finn. I am my father's son. I don't take risks. Risks are scary.

Although I did enjoy all that ice cream.

So maybe tomorrow I'll shake things up a little. Drop in on some classes that aren't on my regular schedule. That'll be a good thing to do. Tomorrow. If I'm still here tomorrow.

Anyhow, like always, when it's first period I head into Mrs. Kimery's class. She teaches science.

Mrs. Kimery starts by asking if anyone has any questions about me! Finn McAllister! My death. How they're feeling about it. She wonders if anybody has anything they need to talk about?

And, wow, people do. I'm kind of surprised. I never realized that so many kids in this class even knew who I was. A lot of their questions are the same ones I've been asking.

Why did it happen? How did it happen? Is my family going to be okay?

People say some pretty nice things about me. It kind of chokes me up. I didn't realize that half of these people even knew we had class together. The heartwarming bubble is burst when the class clown, a girl named Nancy Lombardo, wonders if maybe the school should close for a week in my memory.

Mrs. Kimery glares over the top of her glasses at her.

"Never mind," Nancy apologizes. Then she sinks down into her seat.

To be honest, it's a little embarrassing being the center of attention—first out in the halls, now in my old classroom. I look around the room. Trying to find a distraction from the discussion. And, of course, my eyes land on the life-size skeleton model Mrs. Kimery has at the front of her science classroom. In my current state, it's not something I really want to look at for very long.

So I stare out the windows that face this garden the school has in its central courtyard. It's like a small, boxed-in park with a few trees, a path, and a couple benches. Classes go out there sometimes to measure rainfall, plant seeds, or check on butterfly feeders.

But it's not the butterflies that catch my eye.

It's this girl. I kind of recognize her.

I think her name is Isabella.

Isabella Rojas.

Right. Four months ago, Isabella Rojas was the one everybody was talking about, not me. Her name and face were everywhere—including billboards. Four months ago, she was our state's most famous missing child. To this day, nobody knows what happened to her.

Except maybe me.

Because I just saw Isabella Rojas walk through a tree.

Uh-oh. Today's topic is me.
And I don't know the answers.

CHAPTER 21

THAT'S RIGHT.

Isabella Rojas's a freakin' ghost, just like me.

While I'm looking at her through a window on the south side of the courtyard, she has her face up against a classroom window on the east side of the garden.

Curious, I slip out of Mrs. Kimery's classroom by walking through the wall with all the windows. The class turtle bowl sitting on the windowsill passes right through my stomach. My approach is absolutely silent. I make less noise than the wind rustling through the trees.

I drift up behind the girl. She has long, straight hair. It's jet black. She's also wearing a knitted ski cap and a sweater. Because she was reported missing back in February. Now it's June. Nobody wears a ski cap in June unless they're a barista at a coffee place.

She leans forward, her face passing through a windowpane.

I don't want to startle her but, like I said, I'm curious. Is she really a fellow ghost? Can I talk to her? If I do, will she hear me?

Of course, I'm afraid to find out the answer to all those questions but I screw up my courage as best I can and say, "Uh, hey."

She whips around, pulling her face out of the glass. It goes momentarily taffy-ish during the spin but pulls itself back together. Her chocolate-brown eyes are wide open. She looks freaked.

Congratulations, Finn, I think. *You've officially done your first spooking as a ghost.*

"Wh-wh-who are you?" she sputters in a voice that's so quiet I almost don't hear it.

"Finn McAllister," I say, giving her a jaunty two-finger salute. I don't know why. Maybe I'm nervous. Anyhow, the salute felt like a good idea at the time. (It probably wasn't.)

She takes a few steps back. Enough to be halfway buried in the wall of the school. I think my little salute spooked her, too.

I open up my arms to let her know there's nothing to be afraid of.

"I'm dead!" I try to explain. (This might be the first time that expression has ever been used to calm someone down.) "I can walk through trees!"

Now she's giving me a very quizzical look.

"Trees?" she says.

I gesture over my shoulder. "Like you just did. You're Isabella, right? Isabella Rojas?"

"Yes."

"You disappeared back in February, right?"

She closes her eyes like she's ashamed and nods.

"So, what're you doing still hanging out at school?"

She shrugs. "That's a very good question." There's a long pause as her eyes drift around, taking in all our surroundings.

"You were in the eighth grade, right?" I ask.

"You certainly have a lot of questions," she says with a sly smile. "Maybe you should've asked me a few before I vanished."

"Yeah. Sorry."

She shrugs. "I was as invisible back then as I am right now."

"So, are you, uh, checking in with your friends? That's what I've been doing. Hanging around my friends."

She gives me a look. "I didn't have any friends. Remember? You weren't the only one who never said *boo* to me when I was alive."

"Oh." I am stunned. Even I had four friends and I'm a nerd! "Zero?"

"Zip. I always sat alone in the cafeteria. Hid in the back of the class. Never did any teams or extracurricular activities."

"So, uh, if you don't mind me asking: Why are you here? I mean, I know why you're *here*. Because you're a ghost. Duh. Like me. But why are you hanging out at school?"

She shrugs. "It feels safe. Familiar. I mean I can't go home. Not after what I did. And I'm afraid to move on to whatever comes next. What if I don't have any friends there, either?"

In a weird way, I'm almost tempted to say, *Hey, I'll be your friend. We have a lot in common. After all, we're both dead.*

But—nah.

Who knows what scary stuff that might lead to?

We should start an after-school club together: The Dead Kids.

CHAPTER 22

"UM, LOOK," I tell her. "I'd love to hang with you but, uh, I have some unfinished business to take care of."

Actually, I just have so many problems of my own, I don't really want to deal with whatever hers might be.

"I need to, you know, go finish some junk. Business, and whatnot."

"Yeah," says Isabella, staring down at her canvas sneakers. The tops, I notice, have spiraling doodles all over them. "Me, too. Unfinished business."

Whoa, I think. *She disappeared four months ago, and probably died then, too. And she's still not done with whatever she needed to get done? Her business is still unfinished?*

How is that possible?!?

But I don't ask any of those questions. I just say, "Oh, cool. Got it. Awesome."

Yes, I've always had such a way with words when talking to girls who aren't Annie.

"Yeah. Cool." Isabella is almost as brilliant a conversationalist as me.

Anyway, she goes her way and I go mine.

I know I'm supposed to be investigating what happened up on Ridge Rim Road, tracking down my killer, but, to be honest, right now being a ghost is just too, I don't know, interesting. I can't seem to focus on my main mission. There's too much stuff I always wanted to do at school but never did.

For instance, I could check out the girls' bathroom. No. Wait. That's too creepy and skeevy. Even for a ghost.

But, I could go check out the forbidden zone known as the Faculty Lounge. I've always wondered what goes on in there? So I slip through the wall from the hall, passing through a few more lockers, and check out the legendary teacher hangout.

Okay. Get this—the teachers have *two* vending machines! Pop *and* snacks. They also have a refrigerator. I stick my head through the fridge door and see lots of plastic containers labeled with names. Looks like Mrs. Kimery is having some kind of Thai noodle leftovers for lunch today. The teachers also have a microwave, a coffee maker, a half-empty box of doughnuts, and all sorts of fun mugs. It's a wonder any of them ever want to go home.

One of the doughnuts in the box is coated with powdered sugar. My fave.

If I take a nibble, will anybody notice? Actually, I could probably eat the whole thing and teachers will just think some other teacher grabbed it and gobbled it down.

I reach for it.

Suddenly, it's a frosted doughnut. As in covered with an icy frost instead of white sugar. It looks like something from the inside of a freezer in serious need of defrosting. Seeing the doughnut, I'm reminded of the chills I gave to Annie. And Frank Dussendorf.

Yes, I was able to eat ice cream. But it was already frozen.

Interesting. Is this my ghostly super power? Freezing stuff like that guy Iceman who hangs with the X-Men?

I see Mr. Skaggs's name taped to one of the mugs. It's the dullest on the shelf. Because he's the dullest—not to mention meanest—teacher in the school.

I look at the frosty doughnut.

I look at Mr. Skaggs's mug.

I have a funny, if slightly wicked, idea about how to liven things up in his classroom!

CHAPTER 23

I ZOOM THROUGH the faculty lounge windows, fly across the courtyard, and hang a Louie through the brick wall so I can seep into Mr. Skaggs's math class.

Mr. Skaggs is, of course, at the front of the class, working some kind of geometry problem on the whiteboard. He speaks in a monotone. Mickey used to joke that "Skaggs was a hypnotist before he became a teacher. That's why he's so good at putting people to sleep."

Christopher and Annie are both in his third-period class. Mr. Skaggs is drawing a bunch of intersecting lines. And dotting them. And adding letters to identify the points. He does all of this very, very slowly. With equally slow narration.

". . .this is point 'G.' And this is point 'H.' I'm not going to label a point 'I' because it might look like an 'L' and cause confusion. I will not use a 'J' for similar reasons. . ."

Christopher is yawning. Annie looks drowsy. Her head

jerks back every time she snaps out of her daze and tries to stop her chin from hitting her chest.

Mr. Skaggs drones on. "Instead, I will skip to 'K.' And 'L,' because I didn't use 'I' or 'J'..."

Somebody needs to perk up Mr. Skaggs.

So, I stand beside him, smile, and take a giant step sideways. I pass right through him.

"The lines all intersect at...brrr...brr."

He shivers and shimmies his head like I just gave him a brain freeze. But he keeps going.

"The measure of angle GNF is—"

I step through him again.

"S-s-sixty degrees."

His teeth chatter.

"And the measure of—"

This time I leap through him.

"An-an-angle M-m-m-N-n-n-L-l-l..."

His whole body is quivering. It's like he's trying to teach math outdoors during a blizzard in his underwear. My friends are smiling. The whole class is paying attention. This is the most entertaining Mr. Skaggs has ever been!

"Is it cold in here?" he suddenly asks. "Or is it me?"

No! I want to say. *It's me!*

I hop through him again and land with a dramatic flourish like I'm a ballerina. Mr. Skaggs does a full body tremor. He's shaking so much, he drops his dry-erase marker. The

Now that I'm dead, I'm the life of the party!

classroom is cracking up. Some kids are even applauding. Yes, I'm quite the entertainer, now that I'm dead.

Of course I never would've done anything so bold back when I was, you know, alive. Too risky. Mickey was the only one I knew who could get away with pulling pranks in a classroom. He'd mastered the classic finger-flick-to-the-cheek drip sound effect. And even when he got caught, his smile was so charming the teachers would just laugh.

In fourth period, I go to social studies. Because Ms. Stubblefield is an awesome teacher. She can make anything interesting. Even the Cold War, which is kind of what I just waged on Mr. Skaggs. I hover off to the side and it hits me: I'm going to miss Ms. Stubblefield and everything she still had to teach me.

I'm also never going to go to high school. Or college. There is so much I will never learn.

Bells ring and it's time for lunch.

Bummed, I float through the wall and head down the hall, weaving my way through a mob of eighth graders.

Some of them shiver.

Because I accidentally slide through them, too.

CHAPTER 24

MR. MOONEY, the principal, the guy who came to my funeral, is standing outside his office looking stern and telling
the eighth graders streaming through the corridors to the
cafeteria to "slow down" and reminding them that "there's
no running in the hallways."

I stand beside him and make some pretty funny
angry-principal faces. He clasps his hands behind his back,
I clasp mine behind my back. I waddle like I'm a penguin.
Mr. Mooney doesn't see me making fun of him. Neither does
anybody else. I think about jumping through him, repeating
the shiver show I put on in Mr. Skaggs's class, but, to be honest, I'm starting to feel like a one-trick pony.

Doing the one thing I can do, over and over, is kind of
boring. So I quit making funny faces and silly principal poses.
Mr. Mooney, however, keeps going.

He calls out a few individuals by name. Including
Christopher.

"Mr. Owens?"

Christopher stops. Looks at his feet.

"Yes, Mr. Mooney?"

"Please look at me when I'm speaking to you."

"Yes, sir." Christopher raises his eyes. Slightly.

"I'm sorry to hear about your friend Quinn."

"Finn."

"Excuse me?"

"His name was Finn. Finn McAllister."

Mr. Mooney looks at a note card he has tucked in his shirt pocket. "Right. Finn. My apologies."

Wow. He came to my funeral but doesn't even know my name? Come on. It was printed right on the program. Man. I really *was* invisible at this school long before I fell off that cliff and became a ghost. I was just like Isabella Rojas. Except I had Christopher, Annie, Axe, and Mickey. Four, count 'em, *four* friends!

"If there is anything any of us can do..." says Mr. Gooney. I mean Mooney. Hey, if he can forget my name...

"Thanks," says Christopher. "I'm good. We're, you know, coping as best we can."

That's Christopher, the A-plus student. He copes with stuff other people only deal with.

But the way he says it? This hasn't been easy on him. We were friends. Good friends. Best friends. We were the Nerd Brothers. Now I can still see him but he can't see me. It's not fair.

Man, I wish I'd never gone bike riding up on Ridge Rim Road.

I slump my shoulders and follow Christopher into the caf.

"What's the matter, Owens?" cracks Frank Dussendorf from his table where he is surrounded by grinning goons. "Sad because your girlfriend died?"

Christopher narrows his eyes.

Axe is beside him in a flash.

"Come on, Christopher," says Axe. He's so huge, he casts a shadow over Frank Dussendorf and half of his table. "Don't let Dussendorf get under your skin."

"Yeah," adds Mickey, swaggering over to give Christopher even more support. "I mean, check it out. The guy still drinks juice out of a box."

Annie comes over, too. "Maybe we should chip in and buy you a sippy cup, Frank."

My friends cluster around Christopher (who's smiling now) and escort him over to a table. Our table.

"Losers," Dussendorf mutters to his clump of friends. "Besides, this juice box? It was given to me, for free, by a very grateful sixth grader."

"What were they so grateful about?" grunts a guy named Logan who always sits with Dussendorf at lunch.

"That me and my big brother Joe didn't kill 'em. They tried to use our toll road without paying."

His buddies all snort and chuckle.

Dussendorf takes a sip of his juice box. Don't ask me why,

but for some reason I decide to give the cardboard container a strong blow. It's true—I can't breathe (don't need to) but, as it turns out, I can still exhale pretty good.

The juice box goes frosty.

Dussendorf's cheeks collapse. It looks like he's trying to suck an ice cube through a teeny-tiny straw.

The Cold War continues!

My next stop? The Dussendorf house.

I really need to see if Frank's big brother, Joe, drives a black van.

CHAPTER 25

BUT FIRST...

Yeah. I'm having a lot of *but firsts* (because these will most likely be my *last* days on earth).

I think I'm still mad at my dad for blaming me for what happened up on Ridge Rim Road when, maybe, he should be blaming the Dussendorf brothers. Those guys could be the real villains.

So, on my way to check out Frank and Joe's driveway, I take a little detour. I jump cut myself downtown to my father's office. I stand on the sidewalk for a while, staring up at the big glass skyscraper. Several people pass through me. They, of course, shiver. One gets the chills so bad she sneezes. I'm kind of afraid to float up to Dad's office on the twenty-third floor. In fact, I stand there staring up so long, a hot dog cart rumbles through me (and loses some of its steam).

I wonder if my father still blames me.

Maybe he's found a new statistic. I remember some of the

ones he hurled at me when I first got my Tony Hawk bike. "Males are far more likely to be involved in cycling accidents than females. Children aged ten to fifteen are more at risk than other age groups because children in middle school often start exhibiting riskier behavior."

Yeah. Dad knew how to make anything less fun.

I sigh and decide to walk up to his office. Yes, I could float up twenty-three floors and pass through the mirrored glass walls but I'd need to keep my eyes shut the whole time.

So, I stroll through the revolving doors (without revolving them) and get on an elevator with a guy. He's the only one in the car. He taps a number. This is my lucky day. He's going up to twenty-three, too! If he was going higher than me, there'd be the whole embarrassing moment when he wondered who the heck asked the elevator to stop at twenty-three but didn't get on.

When the door slides shut, the man waits until we've traveled two floors before ripping a very loud fart. Gross. This is when I wish my sense of smell had died when I did. The guy, on the other hand, has a satisfied look of relief on his face.

We reach twenty-three. I wait for the doors to glide open and notice the grimace on the face of the lady stepping in to ride the elevator down. Her eyes are watering. I'm glad she can't see me. There's only one person to blame. The guy who ate too many bean burritos last night.

I bet that lady is wishing
she was dead right now, too!

I glide past the reception area and pass all sorts of very serious-looking accountants and actuaries and insurance salespeople. Men and women in white shirts or blouses and dark suits.

I've never been to my dad's office before. So I have to study the names on the tiny, uniform placards attached to the glass windows outside the beige-colored doors. I know Dad isn't in a cubicle because we had a minor celebration (vanilla ice cream, two scoops each) when he moved up to an actual office.

I find "McAllister" etched into a brown plastic door marker. Dad isn't in his office. I drift inside and check it out anyway.

There are thick statistics books neatly arranged on top of a filing cabinet behind his desk. He also has a pretty cool-looking phone with lots of buttons. There are two framed photos. One is our most recent Christmas card family portrait. The other is a bunch of guys. All of them in camouflage fatigues. They're posing in a desert in front of a military truck that has a Bart Simpson doll strapped to its radiator grille.

One of the guys looks like a much younger version of Dad.

I hardly recognize him. Especially the smile on his face.

Huh. I never knew that my father was in the army.

I guess we all have secrets.

CHAPTER 26

SO THAT'S ANOTHER MYSTERY for another day.

Since Dad isn't in his office, I flit over to the Dussendorf house. When I land in their driveway, I sense that somebody is watching me, which is an extremely unusual feeling because nobody can see me so how can they watch me?

I shake the feeling off and begin snooping around. There are no cars parked on the asphalt. So I walk through the garage door to see if anything is inside.

There is, of course. A ton of landscaping equipment, a workbench, mountains of boxes, and, there, parked in the center of all the mess, sits a van!

A *white* minivan. The kind a soccer mom might drive if her sons kicked things besides other people's children.

But I'm looking for a *black* van. Chances are, if Mrs. Dussendorf has a white van, Mr. Dussendorf doesn't drive a black van. And I think I can safely assume that Joe, the older brother, doesn't have a car or van of his own, otherwise he and Frank wouldn't walk to school every morning. If you own a car when you're in high school, you definitely drive it to show it off. Unless, you know, you inherited your parents' old station wagon. The old station wagon you try to hide.

The Dussendorf brothers drop down several places on my Possible Van Driving Psycho list. My bigger problem? Nobody else is even on that list.

Before I slip out of the garage, I run a little experiment. I touch the rear windshield with my fingertip. Whoa! It left a frosty circle. It fades away after a few seconds but I was definitely able to make a temporary mark in the non-dead world.

I make two dots, draw a circle around them, and give my stick figure man a huge smile.

I have created my first frosty smiley face.

A few seconds after I remove my finger from the glass, the image vanishes.

But, who knows? Spelling something frosty with my fingertip might come in handy. Especially if I need to tell the police who ran me off the road so they can go tell my father!

Feeling kind of pumped after discovering this primitive form of communicating with the living, I glide out of the garage and into the driveway.

Once again, I have the feeling that somebody is spying on me.

It's Isabella Rojas. The other ghost kid.

I see her in the next-door neighbor's yard but pretend like I don't. She's doing a terrible job of hiding behind a tree. I can see strands of hair on either side of the tree trunk.

I guess Isabella's curious about me.

I can't blame her. It's been four months since she disappeared and she still doesn't have any friends, dead or alive. But I'm not looking for a new bestie. I'm looking for a maniac in a black van.

I decide to ignore Isabella and head back to the scene of the crime. BOOM! Just by thinking about it, I'm back on Ridge Rim Road.

I keep my eyes glued to the black asphalt as I climb up that steep hill to the summit—the spot where I actually took the plunge over that retaining wall. I'm looking for skid marks. Tire tracks. Unfortunately, I see a ton of them but I don't know what any of them can tell me about the van I'm looking for—or if any of this physical evidence has anything to do with the one motor vehicle in the world that I'm searching for.

Frustrated, I look up.

I'm maybe ten yards away from the place where I went flying over the low stone wall, and you won't believe what I see.

Not just the mounds of flowers, rows of candles, clumps of balloons, and piles of stuffed animals that people have placed on the ground in front of the shrubs to mark the place as a memorial. That's pretty amazing, sure. But what's even more incredible?

My dad is there, too.

Yes, folks, when I was little,
I used to sleep with Mr. Flopsy-Wopsy.
But I quit doing that when I got older.
Last year.

CHAPTER 27

DAD TUCKS THE OLD stuffed rabbit I used to sleep with between a teddy bear and a bunch of white roses.

And, yeah, his name is Mister Flopsy-Wopsy. Because of the ears. Never mind.

Anyway, this is why Dad wasn't at the office. He wanted to come up here and visit my makeshift memorial.

"I miss you, Finn," he whispers. "But I can't understand why you'd do something so—I'm sorry, son—stupid. Was it peer pressure? Did one of your friends make you do this? Because research shows that teens are much more likely to take risks when other teens are around. And you *were* thirteen..."

Whoa. Now I really, really, *really* need to find out the truth about the van that ran me over this cliff. Dad's starting to blame my friends for what happened to me.

"That's sweet," says a soft voice behind me. "Your father remembered your favorite childhood friend."

I turn around.

It's Isabella Rojas.

"What was the bunny's name?" she asks.

"None of your business."

"Pretty weird name for a stuffed bunny."

"Why are you following me?" I snap.

Her eyes widen. Like she's afraid I might lash out at her, which, duh, I guess I kind of just did.

"Um, I'm not sure," she says. "It's been so long since I talked to anybody who could talk back to me. I'm sorry. I thought maybe you needed somebody to talk to, too."

"Look," I tell her. "My father and I are having a moment." I gesture to indicate my dad.

But he's not there anymore, and all of a sudden, it's twilight.

Apparently, we've jumped ahead on the timeline. I'm not sure if I triggered it or if Isabella did, but the sun is disappearing beyond the pines to our west. It must be eight or nine o'clock at night. Dad's gone home and has already finished dinner.

"Great. Now my father's gone." I give Isabella a look. "You followed me to Frank and Joe's house, too, right? I saw you trying to hide behind that tree. Your hair was sticking out."

While she nervously smooths down her hair, I stare. I mean, I stare *hard*. Because I still can't believe I'm talking to a freaking ghost—something I can only do because I'm a freaking ghost, too!

"I'm sorry I bothered you," says Isabella. She glances down into the ravine. Down to the jagged rocks a hundred feet below.

"Yeah," I tell her. "That's where I died."

She looks at me like she wants to tell me a secret.

But then, she changes her mind I guess.

Because she runs away! She tears down the hill in a blur. I follow after her. Where the heck does she think she's going? I may be dead, but you can't just sneak up behind me, strike up a conversation, and then run away.

I fly down the hill after her. I realize, I *do* need to talk to her!

Isabella has been an apparition longer than me. She might have some tips I can use in my investigation. She might also be faster than me. Because I can't keep up with her, even though I'm whipping along like a flying banshee. She's whipping along like a speeding bullet.

I reach the blinking red stoplight hanging over the intersection at the bottom of the hill. This is why biking up the steep slope of Ridge Rim Road is so hard. You have to come to a complete stop before you can attack it.

I make a right turn. Head down County Route 13. Not sure why. I just have a hunch that this is the way Isabella went.

The sky is darkening. Both sides of this rutted two-lane

blacktop are lined with thick stands of trees. It feels like the kind of stretch of road that a ghost would haunt so they could jump out at passing cars. I squint, but I can't see Isabella.

Until I do.

She's right in front of me and in my face.

CHAPTER 28

SHE LEAPED OUT of the darkness.

I slammed on the brakes. I might've had a heart attack if I still had a heart that was thumping inside my chest. Isabella and I are in a stare-off, hovering over the middle of the deserted road. We're alone. Except for the crickets.

"Why are you following me?" she demands.

"I asked you first," I counter. "Remember?"

"When?"

"Oh, about a minute ago."

"If you don't leave me alone," she says, "I'm going to scream."

I shrug. "Go ahead. Scream away."

And that's exactly what Isabella does. Very loudly. But nobody can hear her except me. Not even the group of deer nonchalantly crossing the highway.

Now I wish Mickey were here with me. Not that I wish he were dead. It's just that Mickey knows how to talk to girls who aren't Annie. Me? Not so much.

"Okay," I tell Isabella, holding up both hands to show I come in peace. "Calm down."

"Calm down?" She's still kind of screaming.

"Just chill. I'm on your side. We're on the same team. We're the dead kids." I shake my fists like I'm a cheerleader with a pair of invisible pom-poms. "Go, Dead Kids!"

She glares at me.

I mime another pom-pom shake. Finally, she grins. I lower my hands and casually tuck them into my jeans pockets, like Mickey would do to look cool.

"So, where are you headed next?" Isabella asks.

"I don't really know. I should probably go to the police. Sometime. I don't have anything to tell them, though. Not yet, anyhow. Oh, hey—have you tried that thing where you touch glass and it frosts up?"

She nods. "I spooked an entire busload of kids. I tapped on the rear exit window. It did not end well. Lots of screaming and a panicked dash for the front door."

That makes us both laugh a little.

"I figure that's how I'll communicate with the cops," I tell her. "But without the screaming and the panicking. Once, you know, I have something to tell them."

"About what?"

"My killer."

"Really? Someone killed you? Like a murderer?"

"Definitely. Technically, it was probably more manslaugh-

If a ghost screams in the woods and nobody hears her, is she still dead?

ter than murder. I was out biking and they ran me off the road and over the cliff up there on Ridge Rim Road."

"That's horrible."

"I know. I was there. Hey, how about you? How'd you, you know, 'pass'?"

That scared look crosses her face again. "I don't remember."

"You don't remember?"

"I used to. When, you know, it first happened. Now it all seems so long ago."

Um, hello, I think. *It was only four months ago. We're talking February.*

But then I realize forgetting stuff probably comes with being dead. You don't need everything you needed when you were alive. You start dropping baggage.

But I sort of like my baggage. Especially the suitcases with my friends in them.

"So," I ask, trying to chitchat like I've seen Mickey do. "Do you live around here?"

She smiles softly. "Not anymore."

"Right," I laugh. "Me neither."

"I used to live on Oak Street. I remember that."

"Sure," I say. "I know Oak Street. I'm on Birch. I mean. . ."

"You *were* on Birch."

"Right. I bet you go visit your house a lot, huh?"

Isabella shakes her head. "No. I've never been back."

"Seriously? Never? That was one of the first things I did."

Isabella sighs. "I'm afraid of what my parents must think of me."

"Why?"

"I can't remember that, either. Just when I think about visiting them, I start to tremble. The fear is overwhelming. It just scares me so much. . ."

"Is that why you hang out at the middle school?"

"I guess. I never had any friends at school but it feels familiar. Not as scary as home would be. And I like the butterfly garden. I think the butterflies can see me."

"Well, I'm going to find out who did this to me," I tell her.

"I know what happened. Now I just need to dig up the deets. Especially whodunit."

Isabella nods. "I wish I could just remember *what* happened to me. Then I wouldn't be so afraid to go say good-bye to my family."

"Well, maybe that's why we're still hanging around. Why you followed me and I followed you. Maybe we're supposed to help each other finish our unfinished business and move on. Not that I mind hanging around. Or hanging out. With you. I mean, not so far, anyway."

She smiles again. "Thanks. I think."

We both laugh again. It feels extremely good to laugh with someone other than the crickets.

Isabella gives me a look. It's a nice one. "I like hanging out with—"

BOOM!

Isabella gasps.

Probably because Grandpa just popped in.

CHAPTER 29

"IT IS TIME!"

Isabella retreats a few steps. "Who's he?"

"My grandfather," I tell her.

"Is he always this grouchy?"

"Hey, cut him some slack. He's dead. And he's been doing it longer than us."

"Sorry, sir," says Isabella. "No disrespect."

Grandpa McAllister grimaces. "Who is this girl?"

"She's Isabella Rojas," I say. "She disappeared back in February and, well, she's also dead. Now."

"It all happened back in February," Isabella explains. "I think. I keep forgetting details. . ."

"Is that going to start happening to me?" I ask my grandfather. "Will I start forgetting all the details of my life?"

Grandpa completely ignores me. His eyes aren't even really looking at me. They're all milky and glowy and staring off into some foggy space slightly above my head.

"I have come to escort you, Finnegan," he announces. "You are family. Follow me."

He turns around. Another tunnel of light encircles his silhouette.

"It is time!" he bellows. Again. (He really does repeat himself. A lot.)

He starts marching into the light. "Follow me, Finnegan."

I turn to Isabella. She looks terrified.

"Don't be afraid," I tell her. "He's just my guide spirit."

"Why hasn't someone come to guide me?"

"Well, maybe they did and you just forgot."

"I'm scared, Finn! I keep forgetting so much. And your grandfather is totally creeping me out."

"Yeah. Me, too. Little bit. But remember what Christopher's mom said: 'Fear is the true enemy.'"

"Who's Christopher?"

"My very best friend."

"Well, his mother is right. Fear is totally kicking my butt right now."

Grandpa's silhouette is halfway down the tunnel before he finally realizes I'm not following him.

He turns around.

"Finnegan." It's an order this time. A demand. "Come. Follow me. Now!"

He sounds so stern. Worse than Dad on his worst day.

I glance at Isabella. She's trembling.

"Don't leave me," she whispers. "Please? Being alone is even worse than being dead."

"Finnegan?" Grandpa is shouting now. "Follow me!"

I grit my teeth and say something I probably should've said to somebody years ago.

"No, sir."

There is a long, awkward silence.

Grandpa finally breaks it. "Excuse me?"

"I'm not coming with you, sir," I tell him. And then, who knows why, I reach out and take Isabella's hand. "I'm staying here until Isabella and I both finish our unfinished business. No matter how long it takes."

"Final warning. If I leave now, I won't be coming back again."

I nod. "That's cool. I understand. You probably have other souls to guide. . ."

Grandpa McAllister raises both his hands high, like he's the priest blessing his congregation at the end of a service.

"You are on your own, Finnegan McAllister. You are on your own."

He turns and walks away. The light dims. Grandpa vanishes like the morning mist.

Isabella squeezes my hand a little harder. "He's wrong, Finn," she whispers. "You're not on your own. We're in this thing together."

CHAPTER 30

GRANDPA MCALLISTER is gone.

Probably forever.

It's just me and Isabella standing there on the dark country road. Neither one of us says anything. We drop each other's hands. I think we're both lost in our own thoughts.

Me? I'm thinking about that thing Christopher's mother said. The snippet I just replayed for Isabella: "Fear is the true enemy." Mrs. Owens was right. Unfortunately, it was an enemy that I let conquer me for my whole life.

And now for my whole death.

If I'm being honest, I've been afraid to learn the truth about what happened up on Ridge Rim Road. I think that's why I've been stalling. Goofing around at school. Visiting my dad's office. Hanging with Isabella. Hoping there was an easy answer like the Dussendorf brothers are to blame.

Who wanted me dead?

Who ran me off the cliff?

Who should take the blame? Because I have to show my father what happened wasn't my fault or my friends' fault.

"Thank you for staying," says Isabella.

"No worries," I tell her because I've heard Mickey say that to girls. I don't add the wink Mickey usually does. "Maybe we can help each other. I don't think either of us can move on until we finish our unfinished business, so maybe we can do it together."

"Cool. I'd like that, Finn."

Then the strangest of strange things happens (and don't forget, this whole being dead thing is already super strange).

I'm sucked into a flashback. It's like a swirling whirlpool that plops me down in a totally different place at a totally different time. Isabella doesn't flash back with me.

It's not night anymore. It's midafternoon. I'm on my own. Biking up Ridge Rim Road. Again. Pumping hard to climb the steep slope.

I'm reliving the last seconds of my last day.

I look over my shoulder.

There's that hulking black van racing up the road, straight at me.

I can't make out the driver. They're only a silhouette. There's a split-second flash of light, as if somebody snapped a selfie. In that instant, I can see it's a man. An older man. He's wearing a cap. A trucker's hat? Maybe.

The creepy black van pulls closer. Closer.

It's like déjà vu all over again.

I can't quite read the license plate. I know it's a Minnesota tag. I've seen them all my life. 10,000 LAKES is written across the bottom.

The first letter is an M.

The gap is shrinking between the van's front bumper and my rear tire.

The second letter is a V.

I can feel the fear tingling through every inch of my body.

The panic pushing my heart to beat faster. I have never been more afraid.

The third letter is an S.

I freak out, close my eyes, and brace for the impact I know is coming.

But I don't fly off the cliff.

When my breathing slows, I carefully open my eyes.

I'm back on County Route 13 with Isabella. It's night again.

She looks as terrified as I feel.

"You okay?" she asks.

I want to say, *Not really. I'm dead, remember?* But I don't.

"Yeah," is what I say instead.

"What just happened?" she asks. "It's like you were here and not here at the same time."

"I'm not sure," I tell her. "But I think I just picked up my first piece of actual evidence!"

CHAPTER 31

"EVIDENCE?" she says.

"This is my unfinished business. Finding out who ran me off the road. Somehow, I went back in time and became a witness to my own murder. I saw who did it."

"Who?"

"A creepy old man in a creepy black van."

"Somebody you know?"

"I don't think so. I mean, I didn't recognize the guy. Of course, I only saw his face for a split second. There was some kind of flash. He looked old. Like sixty or seventy. And he was wearing a trucker hat. I don't know many old people who live around here. Except my grandmother McAllister. She's the widow of—"

"That spooky old guy in the tunnel of light. Your guide spirit."

"Right. My other grandparents live in Florida."

"Mine, too," says Isabella. "There are a lot of grandparents in Florida."

"Yeah. Maybe they should change their state slogan from the Sunshine State to the Grandparents' State."

My little joke reminds me of the words printed in blue on the bottom of all Minnesota license plates: "10,000 Lakes."

"I saw the license plate, too. The van's from here in Minnesota. M-V-S. That's the first half, anyway. Then comes the silhouette of the state followed by three numbers. I didn't get the numbers. . ."

This is tougher than Wheel of Fortune. Can I buy a vowel?

"Hey, it's a start," says Isabella, encouragingly.

"Yeah. Too bad the guy didn't have a vanity plate. Something like 'IDIDIT.' He'd be a whole lot easier to spot."

Isabella grins. She has a nice smile. Soft and gentle. I get the feeling she didn't use it very often when she was alive. I wonder what's keeping her stuck here? Does she have a killer to hunt, too?

"How are you going to trace the license plate?" she asks.

"I'm not sure. I mean, I can't go to the police and write M-V-S with my frosty fingertip on the first glass or mirror I find. If I did, they'd totally freak when the letters just randomly appeared like something out of a Stephen King movie. And, even if they don't have a heart attack, they'll have no idea what M-V-S means. Most Valuable Sandwich? I have to engineer some way to quickly communicate that it's a license plate number and that it was on the van that ran me off the road. That's a lot of fingertip writing. . ."

"You'll figure it out, Finn. You seem extremely clever."

"Thanks. And, when I absolutely need to get something done, I can get super focused. You should see me the night before a paper I've had a week to write is due. How about you? You never told me about your unfinished business."

Isabella looks down at her sneakers. The ones with all the doodles sketched on the canvas sides.

"It's, you know, kind of personal. Actually, it's *extremely* personal. I'd rather not talk about it."

"Oh," I say. "Sure. Like a boyfriend you need to say good-bye to or something?"

She shakes her head. "I never had a boyfriend."

"Yeah. Me, neither. I mean, I never had a girlfriend. Somebody I was serious about. I had girls who were friends but, you know, never a *girlfriend*. Actually, I only had one girlfriend. Annie. I might've had a crush on her, but I never told her about it. Now I sort of wish I had."

"There's a lot of stuff I wish I'd done," says Isabella.

"Yeah," I tell her. "Me, too."

We both think about that for a quiet minute. Regrets? We have a few. All the things we left undone that, now, we'll never get to do. Trust me, being dead can be a real bummer.

"M-V-S?" Isabella finally says.

"Huh?"

"The license plate on the van. It started with an M-V-S?"

"Right."

"I'll keep an eye out for it."

"Thanks. Where are you going?"

She shrugs her shoulders. "I don't really know."

"Hey, while you're helping me track down the van, maybe I could help you do whatever you need to do."

"No. It's my unfinished business. I need to finish it myself."

"You sure? I'm happy to help."

"Thank you. But I need to do this on my own. See you around, Finn."

She turns, walks a few feet, and vanishes. She pulls a Grandpa and just fades away.

Girls. I didn't understand them when I was alive.

Still don't get them now that I'm dead.

CHAPTER 32

THE NEXT DAY is a Saturday.

I can tell. There's a sleepy early morning feeling to our small town.

I decide to spend those early hours on Main Street. There are a lot of parked cars. On weekends, people drive their various vehicles into town to do all sorts of errands at the bank, the grocery store, or the barbershop.

I'm hoping a black van with M-V-S on its license plate will be one of those vehicles.

The creepy old man behind the wheel? Even though he was wearing that trucker hat I could see that he had very short hair around the sides. Maybe he gets it cut every Saturday at Vern's Barber Shop.

I have to confess I lose a little of my "solve-this-mystery" focus as I stroll up Main Street on a beautiful early June morning. There are so many small things I never really noticed before. Like the dawn. Before the sun rose, the eastern horizon was these incredible shades of pink and orange I'd never seen before.

The birds seem to appreciate dawn's early light. They start singing and chirping the instant the sky wakes up.

I'm near the diner, right underneath a big exhaust fan that must be connected to the hood over the grill because I can smell bacon. Bacon might be the best smell in the

Was all this here when I was alive, and I just missed it?

world. Even better than movie theater popcorn.

I step through the wall so I can hear the sizzle of pancake batter hitting the hot griddle. And the hash browns. I never appreciated how good shredded potatoes, onions, and peppers could smell when they're cooked all together on top of a little grease.

I do see one van. A black van.

And it's parked right in front of the barbershop, which isn't even open yet.

I hurry up the sidewalk and scoot through the car parked behind the van so I can eyeball the van's rear bumper.

There's no M-V-S on the license plate. There are, however, a clump of those stick figure silhouettes letting me know the van's family has a mom, a dad, two girls, a boy, and a dog. Maybe they're all in the diner ordering pancakes with a side of bacon and hash browns.

I never was an early riser on Saturdays. Or Sundays. Or any non-school day.

My friends are probably all sleeping in, too. Christopher, Mickey, Axe, and Annie.

I think about them, and all of a sudden, I'm flitting from house to house, visiting. Don't ask me how. I just think about it and BOOM! There I am.

Yep. Christopher's fast asleep. The book he was reading last night is lying open on his bedside table.

Mickey's sleeping, too—with a big smile on his face. I

think he's having a dream. I also think it's a good one. And whoa—he sleeps in a hairnet?

I find the same thing up in Axe's bedroom. Not the hairnet. Just Axe totally conked out. He snores like a chain saw.

Suddenly it hits me: my friends are all wasting their lives just like I wasted my life. They need to wake up and, you know, smell the bacon.

Man, oh man, you should never sleep in when the dawn puts on a pink-and-orange light show like the one I saw this morning. Even when it's too cloudy for the sky to turn colors, just the fact that the sun rises up every morning is cause for celebration, because one morning, hopefully like ninety years from now, you won't be there to see it. So soak it in while you can, I want to tell my friends. Don't take anything for granted.

There's so much to see, so much to do, life is so beautiful, it's all so incredible. Yes, I'm getting extremely corny. That's another thing death will do to you. It'll make you appreciate every little thing you forgot to appreciate while you were alive.

Like bacon. And sunrises. And really good friends.

CHAPTER 33

OH-KAY.

This is awkward. My early morning visits continue with another BOOM!

Suddenly I'm in Annie's bedroom! She's asleep. I'm standing at the foot of her bed, watching her snooze. If I wasn't a ghost, I'd definitely be considered a creep right about now.

Again, I'm not sure how I wound up in Annie's room. It just happened. I swear. But Annie is a friend, just like Christopher, Mickey, and Axe. I needed to check in on her, too, I guess. So, here I am.

It's a pretty warm morning so Annie's kicked off the covers. Who knew Annie slept in a pajama set where the bottoms look like running pants and the top is covered with poop emojis? But that's her sense of humor. It's a little twisted.

Uh-oh.

Things are about to get bad.

Annie's stretching. And rubbing her eyes. And waking up!

Did she feel me looking at her? Does she sense that I am here? In her bedroom? Watching her sleep?

She shivers a little. Great. Now that I'm dead, everywhere I go I'm like a human air conditioner.

I know I recently suggested that my friends should all wake up and smell the bacon but not Annie, not right now. Technically, I think what I'm doing is one step worse than sneaking into the girls' bathroom at school.

She hauls herself out of bed and heads over to her dresser where she pulls out a bra and other underwear-looking stuff. She's going to get dressed and I'm going to die again if I hang around any longer, because she can't get dressed if she doesn't get undressed first!

Terrified, I bolt out of the room, shoot straight through the wall, and dart into the hall where Annie's groggy father is heading toward the bathroom. I pass through him and give him the chills. I get the chills, too, because I can't believe I almost saw what I just almost saw. If Annie's dad knew, he'd probably kill me if the psycho van hadn't beat him to it!

I fly down the steps and out the front door.

And by "out," of course, I mean "through."

That was sooooo weird. Not the passing through people, walls, and doors. No. The weirdest part? Seeing Annie's bra. And she wasn't even wearing it; just pulling it out of a drawer.

Doesn't matter. I may not be able to unsee that for the rest of my life. I mean afterlife.

And now I know what's even more terrifying than a helicopter ride: a girl's bedroom first thing in the morning!

"I wear one, too," says Isabella. She's waiting for me on Annie's front lawn. "A lot of girls do."

"TMI!" I tell her. "And how do you even know what I'm thinking about?"

She just shrugs and, basically, ignores my question. "A bra for a girl is just like boxer shorts for a boy. It's just part of our underwear. Or do you wear briefs?"

"I refuse to answer that question! What're you doing here, anyway?"

"I've been following you."

"What?"

Isabella shrugs again and holds up her hands apologetically. "I really don't have any friends of my own to visit. So, I followed you. I was lurking. Over your shoulder. I could feel how much those guys all liked you. It must be nice to have friends like that. They all remember you even though you're gone. You'll live on in their stories. And that boy with the hairnet is kind of cute."

I roll my eyes. Great. Even dead girls swoon over Mickey.

"Annie is very pretty," Isabella says as she looks up to the second story of the house where Annie is at the window. She's fully clothed. Phew. "She's the one you had a secret crush on, right? The girl with the bra?"

"Yeah. But I never told her."

Isabella shakes her head. "What a wasted opportunity."

"I know," I tell her. "I had a lot of those when I was alive."

CHAPTER 34

I'M IN A LITTLE BIT of a daze.

Yes, it's a beautiful spring morning. Flowers are in bloom. The leaves on the trees are that pale green they always turn when they first pop out to celebrate the coming of summer.

But all I can see is Annie. In her room. Pulling a lacy black bra out of a dresser drawer.

"I should probably hang with you for a while," says Isabella as we drift up the street where I used to live. "You look like you're in a little bit of a daze."

I give her a curious look. Can she read my mind?

"So this is the street where you used to live?"

Okay. This is just freaky. She's picking up all my thoughts.

"Yeah. About ten houses up the block. Annie and I used to walk to school together. She'd wait for me, right here on the sidewalk. Every morning. If it started raining, I'd always let her share my umbrella. She usually forgot to grab one on her way out the door. My mom always made sure I left home with the proper gear, no matter the weather, because she knew precisely when the precipitation would start and what the real feel temperature would be. She has an app for that. I think my dad downloaded it for her."

As we continue our stroll, I notice how great newly mown grass smells. I never noticed how good it smelled back when I had to mow our lawn. Plus the sweet green scent was always clouded by exhaust fumes from the mower.

The sun swings up in the sky, like in a time-lapse video clip, and, suddenly, it's the early afternoon. I notice a lot of families in their driveways, loading up their cars with picnic gear and pool floats and everything they need for an afternoon at the Lake. Minnesota may be the land of ten thousand lakes but Lake Naniizaanad is the only one people on my street care about.

"It's Saturday," I tell Isabella. "Everybody's heading to the Lake."

"Yeah," she says. "I remember how, as soon as it got warm enough, everybody on our block would head up there on the weekends, too. I never went."

"Never?"

She shakes her head.

"Why not?"

Now she shrugs. "I don't know. My mom wasn't into outdoors stuff. Too many insects. And I didn't have any friends to hang out with up there."

"Yeah," I say. "That's the only time I'd get to go. When my friends and I rode our bikes up to the cliffs without telling my parents where we were going. If I came home with soaking wet shorts or a dripping bathing suit, I'd just fudge a little and tell them I was taking swimming lessons or a life-saving course at the Y. My father liked those. He hated the Lake."

"How come?" asks Isabella.

Her question triggers another jump cut.

We're in my house. My little brother Charlie is dressed in his swim trunks. He has a diving mask and a snorkel tilted back on the top of his head. Charlie is sulking and pouting because Dad is telling him what Dad told me every perfect lake day.

"I'm serious, Charlie," says Dad. "The Lake is a very dangerous place. When I was about your age, my big sister Connie drowned in that water. It's very deep and very unsafe. She was only twelve. She never saw thirteen."

I've heard the words so often, I'm mouthing them along with Dad.

"That's terrible," whispers Isabella.

"I know," I tell her. "But he says it every time Charlie or I want to head up to the Lake. Then he reminds us we have a six-inch-deep kiddie pool in the backyard."

"No," says Isabella. "I mean it's terrible that his big sister drowned in the Lake."

"Yeah. That, too."

"It probably scarred him for life."

"Oh, yeah. That's probably why my father is severely risk averse."

"Charlie," we hear my father say, "did you know that, on average, 3,536 people die from drowning each year? That's ten deaths per day. And males younger than fifteen, like you, are twice as likely to be involved in a fatal drowning than females."

"Huh," I hear Isabella say. "I did not know that."

"I did," I say. "My dad told me the same statistics. Stand by for the next factoid. The one about lakes. . ."

"And," Dad continues, "eighty percent of deaths in rivers, ponds, and lakes are boys!"

I turn to Isabella. "If I'd been a girl, maybe he would've let me jump in the Lake. Except no, because of Connie. Dad had me so freaked about what might happen, even when I went to the Lake with my friends I never dove in. I just waded in a few feet or sat on the rocks and watched them have fun."

"Your dad was just trying to protect you, Finn," says Isabella.

"I guess. But I think he was also trying to protect himself. From his memories of Connie, the aunt I never knew."

"Maybe she'll be waiting for you," says Isabella. "When, you know. . ."

"I finally move on?"

Isabella nods.

"Yeah. Maybe so. Maybe we could go swimming together. When you're already dead, you really don't have to worry about drowning."

CHAPTER 35

"COME ON," I say after I've seen enough of another typical No-Way-Are-You-Going-to-the-Lake-Today Saturday at my house. "Let's go to the Lake!"

"What?" Isabella looks shocked.

"You said you've never been, right?"

"Right."

"So let's go."

"B-b-but. . ."

"It's what I do with all my friends," I tell her.

"Am I your friend?"

"Yeah," I say. "Sort of."

"Because I'm the only one you can talk to?"

"Maybe. I guess. What does it matter? Come on. You need to see the Lake at least once before you, you know, move on. You have to take its memory with you because, forget Disney World, the Lake is the happiest place on earth."

She smiles. "Okay. If you insist."

"I do. Big time."

"Fine."

My house fades away, and instead of standing in my old kitchen, we're up on the cliffs looking down on Lake Naniizaanad. It doesn't look dangerous at all. It just looks like fun.

"Oh, wow!" says Isabella, trying to take it all in. "Oh, wow!"

She reminds me of how I felt on the very first summer Saturday that I snuck up to the cliffs with Christopher and saw how absolutely magical the place was. The water cascading down the rocks. Sunlight dancing across the Lake's

Where I lived, Go jump in a lake is an awesome idea!

surface. People laughing. Splashing. Floating. Drifting. Having fun.

They're all enjoying life, which, now that I can't do it anymore, I really wish I had spent more time doing while I was alive. That gasp and shiver when you first step or plunge into cold mountain water? That's what they call proof of life.

"This is amazing!" says Isabella. She's beaming. "Can you feel that sunshine on your face?"

"Yeah. It feels good."

"No, Finn. It feels amazing! Are your friends here?"

"Maybe." I turn around. "Yeah. Over there. On that clump of rocks. That was our special spot."

"How come they're not in the water?"

"I don't know."

"Let's go find out."

"Um, okay."

This time, I follow her. We cruise across the cliffs and ease up behind Christopher, Mickey, Axe, and Annie. They're just hanging out in one of the shady spots at the top of the trail. Their bikes are all tipped over, lying on the ground.

"You wanna dive in?" asks Axe.

"Nah," says Mickey. "Not right now. Maybe later."

"That's what you said an hour ago."

"Look, Axe, if you want to go swimming, go swimming."

"Nah," says Axe. "It's no fun unless you guys go swimming, too. So, you want to dive in?"

"I dunno," says Mickey. "Maybe later."

"I can't believe it's only been a week," says Christopher sadly.

"Yeah. Last Saturday was the funeral," says Annie.

"But we went swimming afterward," Axe reminds everybody. "I did that ginormous cannonball."

"So swim if you want to," says Annie.

"Nah," says Axe. "Unless you guys want to swim. It's no fun doing it alone. . ."

"Nothing's been much fun since Finn pulled that stunt on his bike," says Christopher.

"Why'd he have to do that?" Annie kicks at a loose stone near her sneaker.

"Guess we'll never know," says Christopher. "He isn't here to tell us."

It wasn't my fault! I want to scream. *There was this crazy old guy in a black van!* But I know my hollering won't do anything except maybe make another bird chirp.

"It rained on Thursday," Annie mumbles.

"And your point is?" says Mickey.

"Finn wasn't there with his umbrella."

"And he's not here today," adds Christopher.

"It's sunny," says Mickey. "We don't need an umbrella."

"And we don't need to go swimming," says Axe. "Unless you guys want to."

"Nah," says Christopher. "I'm going home."

"Me, too," says Annie.

"Good idea," says Mickey.

"Wait for me," says Axe, picking up his towel.

My friends prop up their bikes and push them down the trail. They're too bummed to even ride.

It's as clear as all that sparkling water down in the Lake.

My death has ruined their lives.

CHAPTER 36

MY FOUR FRIENDS DISAPPEAR.

Soon, in another one of those time-lapse sweeps, so does the sun.

And all the happy people having fun in the Lake. There's no more laughter and the only splashing is being made by the water tumbling down the waterfalls.

"I need to do some thinking," I tell Isabella when the sky fills with stars and she and I are the only ones left up on the rocks.

"Me, too," she replies. "I know a place. It's very comforting. Very easy to think. I went there a lot before I met you. Want to come with me?"

"No, thanks. I think I'll just stay up here tonight. You see that murky swoosh in the sky? That's our galaxy. The Milky Way. You can really only see it someplace super dark, like up here. We're so far from town, there's no light pollution."

Isabella nods and acts like she believes me. I sense she is

reading my mind again and knows my real reason for staying on the cliffs.

I really need to be alone.

Isabella disappears.

It's just me, myself, and I up on the rocks underneath a billion stars. It's so beautiful, it's so peaceful, it's so perfect. Just like always. It was probably perfect before I was born. Maybe before anyone was born.

I remember this one night when I was sleeping over at Christopher's house. We snuck out through his window and rode our bikes up here so we could gaze at the stars. We laid on the rocks, flat on our backs, and stared up at the sky.

Christopher, by the way, is big on astronomy. He knew stuff they hadn't taught us yet in school. He was like a one-person planetarium show.

"It takes about one-point-three seconds for light to travel from Earth to the moon," he told me. "It takes eight minutes for light to travel from the sun to Earth."

"So," I said, "if the sun exploded, right now, we wouldn't know about it for eight minutes?"

"Exactly."

I started fidgeting with my watch.

"What're you doing?" asked Christopher.

"Setting an alarm for eight minutes from now. Just in case."

Christopher laughed. "It would take two whole years for that same sunlight to reach the edge of our solar system. Our galaxy, the Milky Way? It would take one hundred thousand years for light to travel from one edge to the other."

"You're making me feel very small and insignificant," I told him.

"Wait," said Christopher. "I'm not done. The observable universe is home to approximately 350 billion more galaxies, all of them the size of our Milky Way. The observable universe— which means it's the only one we know about, which means there might be others—houses thirty-billion-trillion stars."

Mind. Blown.

"So, basically, our whole planet and all the people on it is just one teeny-tiny speck of sand and the universe is all the sand on every beach on Earth?"

What do all the stars in the sky mean?
Easy. We forgot to pack a tent!

"No," said Christopher. "The universe is bigger than that. But, Finn?"

"Yeah?"

"So far, we're the only creatures who realize how incredible the universe is. Sure, there might be other intelligent life-forms on other planets. Aliens, like in *Star Wars*. But until we find out they exist? We're the only ones we know of capable of enjoying all that this ocean of stars has to offer."

I miss shooting the bull with Christopher on starry nights.

In fact, I'm missing a lot of stuff about my old life—even though I'm still here. Sort of.

But what I miss the most is all the stuff I never did.

CHAPTER 37

I SEE A SHOOTING STAR streaking across the sky.

Its life isn't all that long. It burns brightly for an instant and then, POOF, it's gone. Kind of like me, I guess. I was here for an instant (okay, thirteen years) but now I'm gone. Sort of. Although I'm not so sure I ever burned brightly. I kind of wish I'd cranked up my rockets a little bit and left behind a more dazzling trail.

Christopher told me a shooting star really isn't a star at all. It's a meteoroid, a chunk of rock tumbling through space that hits earth's atmosphere and burns up in a flash. Kind of how I feel. I was here, then I was gone. But not completely.

What's up with that? Why am I still hanging around?

"Because you have unfinished business to attend to!" says a scary voice behind me.

I would've jumped out of my skin except I don't think I really have, you know, skin anymore. I do feel goose bumps tingling up whatever my arms are made of.

I whip around.

It's Isabella.

"Whooo-oooo-ooo," she says, making a scary face and mysterious finger twiddles at me, like all of a sudden she's a Halloween ghost.

"Cute," I mutter when I'm done being spooked by my fellow spook.

She grins. "Were you scared?"

"Uh, yeah. But just wait until I sneak up on you!"

"I'll be ready." She sits down beside me on the rocks. "It's beautiful up here, Finn. Especially at night."

"Yeah. I don't think I ever realized how awesome it is. Everything is so incredible. The stars. This smooth rock we're sitting on. Even those annoying crickets making that annoying noise by rubbing their annoying legs together."

Yeah. I'm sounding corny again. Sorry. Can't seem to help it.

"You think we'll get another shot?" I ask.

"Huh?"

"Do you think we'll get a do-over? You know, do you think that maybe our souls will come back in some other body? Maybe in some other time and place?"

"I dunno. I guess it's possible. Some religions talk about reincarnation. A do-over would be nice. . ."

"I'd want to come back as somebody cool," I say. "I'd like to be a real risk-taker, like Mickey."

146

Isabella arches her eyebrows. "You want to sleep with a hairnet?"

"No." I laugh. "I'd skip that part. I'd just be more 'out there,' you know? I'd climb rock walls and stuff. Sure, I'd use the safety harness, but I'd climb 'em."

"Next time around," says Isabella, "I'd put myself out there, too. I would walk up to an interesting stranger in the cafeteria and say, 'Hi. Is this seat taken?' and then I'd sit my butt down. If I could do it all over again, I'd try to make friends the way you guys all did."

"We were just nerds nobody else wanted to hang with," I tell her. "So, we kind of had to hang out with each other.

I guess that's what friends are. People you can be your nerdy self around, no matter what."

"Wait a second," says Isabella, sounding surprised. "Your friend Mickey is a nerd?"

"Not anymore. But he used to be. Back in elementary school. I'd say he was the nerdiest of us all. Especially in third grade. He was a borderline dweeb."

"Finn?"

"Yeah?"

"For what it's worth, I think you're way cooler than Mickey."

I blink at her. "Seriously?"

"Yep."

"Oh, I get it. Because I'm dead so I'm, you know, 'cold.' This is a body temperature thing."

"No," she says, serious. "I just think you're really nice. And cool."

CHAPTER 38

AFTER SOME MORE STAR GAZING and talking about all the things we're going to miss (soft-serve ice cream cones dipped in chocolate that becomes crispy is a mutual fave), Isabella and I decide to go for a stroll.

Of course, our strolls are anything but normal.

We take two steps toward the path down from the rocks and suddenly we're walking on a sidewalk near the big church with the clock tower. How does this stuff happen? Who knows. It just does. Let's face it: being dead is weird.

"Whoa," I say, glancing up at the clock. "It's three o'clock in the morning."

"So?" says Isabella. "Are you sleepy?"

"No. I really haven't felt sleepy since, I don't know—the night before I died."

"Me, too."

"You want to go watch TV or something?"

She gives me a look. "At three o'clock in the morning? Are you a big fan of infomercials?"

"Not really. That's one thing I won't miss. . ."

"Oh, by the way," says Isabella, "I've already started living my new life."

"Really? Even though you're officially dead?"

"Bad choice of words. I mean I'm trying to do like you said. Be out there. Make new friends."

"Seriously? Because we're like the Invisible Man and Invisible Woman. Makes friendships kind of hard. People can see right through us. . ."

Why do I think all of Isabella's new friends are going to give me the cold shoulder? Oh, right. Because they're dead.

"Come with me." She grabs me by the hand. "There's something I want you to see."

"What?"

"Come on!"

"Um, where are we going?"

"To this place I discovered a while ago but I only started talking to people there after I left you up on the rocks."

"You're talking to people? Are they talking back?"

She grins. "Yep. You'll see. I'll introduce you. They're all right over there."

She points.

At the church graveyard.

CHAPTER 39

I SEE DEAD PEOPLE.

There are all sorts of other ghosts hanging out among the headstones. They seem friendly, but, to be honest, it's still extremely spooky.

"Hello, Isabella," says a man in a flannel shirt. His elbows are propped nonchalantly on a tombstone, as if it were the bar in his favorite neighborhood tavern. "Hey, Joey? This is Isabella. The girl I told you about."

"Sure, sure," says the ghost named Joey. He's casually leaning on the next tombstone to the left. "Welcome to the neighborhood, kid. So, anyway, Fred, like I was saying. There was this one time, back in high school, I had a date with a cheerleader..."

"We should probably move on," Isabella whispers.

"Speaking of high school," says Fred, "I ever tell you about my fastball?"

Joey's not listening to Fred's baseball tale. He's still

talking about the time he dated a cheerleader.

"These two like to relive their glory days," Isabella tells me. "Over and over and over."

"Hey, remember that other time. . ." I hear Joey say.

"Guess they have so many good memories," I remark, "they don't want to leave their lives behind."

We come upon a woman who looks remarkably happy for a dead person.

"Uh, hi," I say, giving her a little wave. "I'm Finn. This is Isabella."

"Hi. You two kids hungry?"

"Huh?"

"There's this great five-star restaurant about ten miles up the road," she says. "Never could afford to go there when I was alive. Now? I'm in there all the time. Filet mignon keeps mysteriously disappearing off plates on their way from the kitchen to the dining room. We can eat all we want and never gain a pound. Then there's the all-you-can-eat breakfast buffet at the Grand Duke Hotel. There's so much food, they never notice when the mountain of eggs or bacon gets a little smaller. Of course, I'm still trying to figure out how to snag one of those omelets made to order since I can't actually order one. The chef never hears me. . ."

Isabella and I drift along through the headstones.

Now it's my turn to whisper.

"There are more headstones than ghosts," I observe. "That

means some of these souls moved on. Why are these spirits still stuck here?"

"We should ask," Isabella suggests.

"Really? You don't think that'd be rude? I mean, we're dead and *we're* still hanging around. My guess is they all have some sort of unfinished business like you and me."

Isabella gives me a look. "Seriously? Read that woman's headstone. Do the math. She's ninety-four."

Isabella shakes her head. "She had over nine decades and didn't finish all her business?"

I shrug. "Guess she should've made a list. But maybe

Whoa. She had a lot of candles on her last birthday cake.

there's something she still needs to take care of. One last mission. A crime to solve, even. Maybe she was out riding her bike and some kind of maniac in a black van with a Minnesota license plate MVS-something-or-other ran her off the road and she has to figure out who it was."

Isabella gives me another look. This one involves arched eyebrows. "She was riding her bike? She's ninety-four, Finn."

"Hey, it happens," I say. "Well, it could happen. Maybe."

"I'll ask," says Isabella, sounding way braver than I remember her being.

She moves to the middle of the cemetery. I hang out near a big concrete angel. Okay, so I actually hide behind its wings.

"Everybody? Hello? Uh, hi. I'm Isabella Rojas. And I'm, you know, dead."

"Hello, Isabella," the dozen ghosts in the graveyard chant in response—even the two guys leaning on their headstones rehashing their glory days.

"Why are you all still here?" Isabella asks. "Why haven't you guys moved on to whatever's next? I'm asking for a friend." She winks at me. "And for myself."

A stern young man steps forward. He's wearing a military uniform. Camo colored.

"Simple," he says. "My death was a mistake."

CHAPTER 40

"WE WERE IN THE DESERT," says the young soldier. "Iraq. I was in a convoy, heading back to base. The vehicle I was driving ran over an improvised explosive device. An IED. But, there were two vehicles in front of me. Two! There were two more behind me. I remember one had a Bart Simpson doll strapped to its radiator grille. Funny the little things you remember, huh? Saw it in my rearview mirror. The bomb should've taken out one of those other vehicles, not me. My death was a mistake."

Whoa.

And I thought my death was the worst one ever. (I guess everybody who dies thinks that.)

"I just have some unfinished business to take care of," says an elderly woman. She's not as old as the ninety-four-year-old lady, but she looks very grandma-ish. "I need to look out for my grandchildren."

Yep, she's a grandma. Nailed it.

"I only died because my furnace had a serious ventilation problem. Carbon monoxide poisoning, I heard them say when I was riding to the hospital in the back of the ambulance. I need to stick around and make sure the same thing doesn't happen to my grandbabies."

"How can you do that?" Isabella asks.

The grandmother looks stunned. "I'm not sure. But, if the time ever comes, I'll think of some way to save them, you bet I will!"

"I'm here for the kids up at the camps," says a middle-aged man with slicked-back hair, a thin mustache, and a big, toothy smile. "See, in life I was an entertainer. Magician. One night, I'm in the middle of my act, somebody lets go of the wrong rope, and KA-BOOM! A sandbag conks me on my head. I've heard of people dying onstage, but this was ridiculous. Now I work the summer campfire circuit. Somebody starts spinning a ghost story, I make it come alive, which is interesting seeing how I'm dead. I've worked up some pretty good haunting tricks. Sound effects. A little poltergeist action. I give them chills. Shivers. It's a blast. I wish I had this much fun while I was alive. So I can't leave. Not yet. It's almost summer. My audience needs me. Those kids around those campfires need me."

"We all have work left to do," says another ghost.

"My son's prayers are keeping me here," says another. "He won't let go, so neither can I."

The majority of dead people agree: It
should never have happened to them.

Every ghost has a reason for not leaving. Some make
sense. Sort of. Others are kind of goofy.

"I didn't like my coffin! I need more padding along the
sides. And a softer pillow!"

"I died too young. I deserve more time on earth."

"They gave me the wrong medicine!"

"I was in the wrong place at the wrong time."

"The other driver had been drinking."

I step out from behind my angel.

"Excuse me!" I say, trying to get everybody's attention.

They quiet down and turn to face me.

"I'm Finn. I'm Isabella's new friend."

"Hello, Finn," they all chant.

"Quick question: How many of you would say that you died during an accident? Something that really wasn't your fault?"

Slowly, all the ghosts, except Isabella, raise their hands.

"Yeah," I say. "Me, too."

CHAPTER 41

WE WERE ALL ROBBED, I realize.

Those of us who died but haven't moved on are still here because life cheated us. We weren't supposed to die when we died. But then a furnace leaked or a sandbag fell or a van drove one of us off the road and our lives were cut short. Shorter than they were supposed to be.

My dad once told me that life expectancy in the United States is 78.93 years. I had 65.93 good years to go. If I moved to Japan, Switzerland, Spain, Norway, or a bunch of other countries, I probably wouldn't've died until I hit my eighties.

But thirteen?

That's not on me. That's on the old man driving the creepy black van.

A few more ghosts drift in to join the crowd. Spirits like Isabella and me who aren't actually buried in this church graveyard.

"This graveyard is like Starbucks for dead people," Isabella tells me. "A place to meet. Hang out. Catch up on all the gossip."

"I recognize that lady!" I say. "That's Ms. Johnson. My first grade teacher."

I rush over to the new arrival. Isabella follows after me.

"Hey, Ms. Johnson. It's me. Finn McAllister."

She squints like she's trying to remember who I am.

"I used to be in your class. At the elementary school. My father wouldn't let me use pencils because they were sharp objects and could poke somebody's eye out?"

"Oh, right. Finnegan. You always had markers. Soft, felt-tip markers. And multiple colors of ink stains all over your hands."

"Yes, ma'am. This is my new friend Isabella. She's dead, too."

"Well, then," says Ms. Johnson with her big smile, "I guess that's something we all have in common."

"If you don't mind me asking," says Isabella. "How'd you... pass away?"

"Oh, I slipped and fell in the bathtub, dearie."

I nod. "The bathroom. Most dangerous room in the whole house. My dad says that every year a quarter of a million people visit emergency rooms because of injuries they get in the bathroom."

"Really?" says Ms. Johnson. "Your dad says things like that?"

"Yuh-huh. He's an actuary. For an insurance company. Fourteen percent of those bathroom injuries happen when people are using the toilet."

"I see. Fortunately, mine was in the tub."

"So you were cheated, too!"

"No, Finnegan. I slipped and fell. It was my fault."

"Still, it was an accident. You should've lived longer. That's why you're still here."

"Is that so? I'd been wondering about that. Thank you, Finnegan. Looks like my student has grown up to become my teacher!"

She says good-bye.

I feel a shiver at the back of my neck and slowly turn around.

The soldier in the desert camo uniform is staring at me.

"Did you say your name was McAllister?" he asks.

"Uh, yes, sir. Finn McAllister."

"And your father—was he, by any chance, Thomas McAllister? From here in town?"

"Yes, sir."

The dead soldier nods. "We enlisted together. He was in my unit. A driver. Like me."

Of course! The Bart Simpson doll tied to the front grille of an army truck! That photo in Dad's office.

"My father was there?" I say. "When you died?"

"He was the lucky one. If it hadn't been me, it might've been him. I remember he hauled me out of the wreckage and tried to revive me. I was already gone but he gave me CPR. My spirit was floating over my body, looking down. He took on enemy fire, but he wouldn't leave my side. Your father was a very brave man."

"I never knew. . .I always thought. . ."

"Maybe that's why I'm still here," says the soldier. "So I could tell you the truth. Your father is a hero. He risked his life to save mine, even though mine was already lost."

My father took a risk?

He did something courageous and dangerous?

I wonder if what happened in the desert was so traumatic he never wanted to do anything risky once he got home.

Couple that with what happened to his big sister years ago at the Lake. . .

Yeah. That's enough to make a guy try to stay safe at all costs. And to protect his family from all possible harm.

CHAPTER 42

WE LEAVE THE GRAVEYARD and the sun comes up.

Only, it's three weeks later. I'm reminded of this old rock song my dad liked to hum along to whenever it came on the radio: *Time keeps on slipping, slipping into the future.* That's exactly what just happened to Isabella and me.

It's the end of June. The leaves on the trees are green-green. The tulips are all gone. The world has turned to summer.

It's been almost a month since my funeral. It's also the last day of school.

"I need to hang with my buds," I tell Isabella. "Check in with them. Make sure they're, you know, doing okay without me. Every year, on the last day of school, we head out to the Lake for our Unofficial Start of Summer celebration. They dive in, splash around, swim out to the deep water. I watch from the shore and guard our cooler full of pop."

"Can I go to school with you?" Isabella asks. "I go there

all the time but I might feel less lonely if I'm with you."

"No worries. Come on. Maybe we can punk Mr. Skaggs again. Give him a brain freeze."

Isabella laughs. "No thanks. I prefer remaining a friendly ghost."

When we arrive at the school (not sure how, as usual; we just do), it's before the first bell. Mickey is out front, surrounded by girls—just like always.

"Maybe you ladies want to hit the Lake with me and my buds later today. Celebrate the start of summer. It's so hot out. . ."

He gives his eyebrows a wiggle when he says it's "hot." The girls giggle.

I feel the need to bust Mickey's chops a little.

So I exhale a big, chilly breath.

"Whoooo," he says, shivering.

"Are you okay?" asks one of the girls. I think she's a seventh grader. I don't know her name. Mickey may not, either.

"Yo, Mick?" Axe strides over. "You look sick, bro."

"I'm f-f-fine."

"Then how come your teeth are chattering?"

"There was a breeze. A really cold breeze."

"Seriously?" Axe looks at the girls. They shrug. "Dude, it's like eighty out."

"So? I feel like I slurped a slushee way too fast."

I think Mickey just caught a summer cold.
From me.

"You think you're coming down with something?" Axe asks.

"No," Mickey protests. "Like I said, it was just a cold breeze."

"Dude? There are no cold breezes anywhere except maybe up at the Lake. We on?"

"Yeah. Right after school. These ladies might join us."

"Yeah," says one of the girls feebly. "We might. Thanks for the invite."

When they're gone, Axe puts his big hand on Mickey's shoulder. "Dude?"

"Yeah," says Mickey. "I know. They're not coming with us."

"You freaked them out, Mickey. You freaked them out, big time. Next time you have a brain freeze, don't do it in public."

Mickey laughs. Axe laughs. I start laughing, too. They head into the school and I tag along like I always would. I love laughing with my friends. It might've been my favorite part of being alive.

Only now they can't hear me. Laughter's not so great when you're doing it alone.

"It's okay, Finn," says Isabella when I stop to let my laughing buddies go on ahead without me. "I thought what you did was funny. They just don't know you're the one who did it."

"Yeah," I say, suddenly feeling extremely sad. "And they never will know. Because I'm not really here anymore."

CHAPTER 43

WHAT FEELS LIKE a minute later, school's out for the summer.

Everyone comes streaming out the front doors screaming. They've all been set free until early September.

"Let's go up to the Lake," says Isabella. "Hang out on the rocks. Maybe this day will turn into night and we can look at all those stars again."

I think she's trying to cheer me up. She's sweet that way.

"Yeah," I tell her. "Good idea."

And, in a flash, we're there! On the rocky cliffs, looking down at the hypnotic waterfalls. Breathing in all the incredible smells. Not having to worry about mosquito bites.

"It's still totally awesome up here," I say.

"It's a very special place," adds Isabella.

"The most special."

The scenery seems to cross-dissolve with itself to a time thirty minutes in the future. My friends appear. They're seated in a circle on a sunny rock. Fidgeting with sticks. Playing with pebbles. Shooting the bull.

"It's too cold to swim today," announces Christopher.

Annie nods. "The water's freezing. At least this rock is nice and warm."

"Yeah," cracks Mickey. "It reminds me of the butt warmers in my mother's car."

They all laugh.

"Yo," says Axe. "Mickey was super cold earlier, though. Like someone had stuck a pair of Popsicles up his nose or something."

Mickey gives Axe a glare. "It was a chill, okay? A chill. Everybody gets them."

"Not today," Annie points out. "It's like eighty degrees."

"Then how come the water is so freezing cold?" wonders Mickey. "On account of the waterfall?"

"Partly," says Christopher, the brainiac. "It actually has more to do with the change of seasons. The bright sun will warm the surface of the Lake but, as we move into summer, winds die down. They aren't strong enough to mix the warmer water on top with the cold water down below, especially out there in the bottomless section of the Lake."

"It's not 'bottomless,' Christopher," scoffs Annie.

"Otherwise," says Mickey, "it would leak out on the other side of the planet."

"Who says it isn't doing that?" remarks Axe. "Maybe the

Lake water goes all the way through the core of the earth and bubbles up in the Pacific Ocean. Somewhere near Hawaii. Maybe that's what causes all those volcanoes. Bottomless lakes here in Minnesota."

"Huh," says Mickey. "That would explain all those geysers and junk out in Yosemite. Those are leaks from bottomless lakes over in Mongolia or someplace."

It's like I'm not even here. Which, okay, I'm not. But still...

Okay. I know what they're saying is ridiculous. Stupid, even. But I miss doing it with them *so much*.

"Anyway," says Christopher, trying to bring the conversation back to some sort of reality, which is what he always has to do, "the sharp temperature difference between the surface water and what's underneath is called a thermocline."

My friends just nod. They're used to Christopher saying nerdy stuff like that. It's what makes him Christopher.

"Hey," says Annie, "did you hear about the weatherman who named a snowstorm after his son Kevin? Yeah, he didn't think the storm was going to amount to much, either."

More laughs.

"You know why England is so wet?" says Axe.

"Easy," says Mickey. "Because the queen has reigned there for decades!"

"Aw, you knew that one. . ."

And so it goes. My friends keep riffing on the weather. Making bad puns. Telling corny jokes. Going off on wild tangents.

And not even mentioning my name.

CHAPTER 44

"I NEED TO LEAVE," I tell Isabella.

"Sure," she says. "They're chatting about the weather. *The weather.* That's what old people talk about. They haven't mentioned you once. Have they forgotten you already?"

I give her a look. Remember that mind-reading stuff she was doing the other day? She's still doing it.

"I want to walk," I tell her. "So don't think about where we should go or POOF! We might end up there."

"Fine. Where do you want to walk?"

"Ridge Rim Road."

"That's where you died."

"Yeah. I know. I was there when it happened."

So, we walk in silence. Down the bike trail from the cliffs. Up the road that will take us over to the other side of the ridge. Neither one of us saying a word. Maybe I don't have to—what with Isabella constantly reading my mind. I'm not really thinking about that right now, though. No, I'm thinking about my life.

I did so little with it.

I was so forgettable. All it took was a few weeks for Annie, Christopher, Axe, and Mickey to move on to a whole new topic. The weather.

The freaking *weather*!

Turns out the most boring discussion topic in the world is more interesting than me.

Does it get any lamer than that?

Yes. It does. Just wait and see.

We continue along Ridge Rim Road and come to the Spot. The scene of the crime. It's now the site of the saddest memorial ever erected on the side of the road. The teddy bears and stuffed animals are tattered and frayed and splattered with mud. Their fur is soaked. The flowers are all wilted stalks topped with dead petals. The paint on the homemade signs has gone runny with the rain. Somebody driving by tossed out a Burger King bag and several paper cups with plastic lids.

No one has been out to tend to the memorial in weeks. It looks like what it is: a trash heap.

My memory is being erased from this world, bit by bit. First my friends, now this.

"I'm so sorry, Finn," Isabella says softly.

"Yeah. Me, too." I think I might've cried except ghosts don't have tear ducts.

Suddenly, we hear a groaning, straining engine.

One I've heard before.

We look down to the bottom of the hill and the flashing red light. A black van comes to a stop. The driver waits for a second and then, engine screaming, roars up the steep hill.

As the monstrous thing comes closer, I see the guy behind the wheel is wearing a trucker cap.

And then I spot the license plate: MVS 472.

It's him. My Stephen King maniac.

174

CHAPTER 45

INSTINCTIVELY, I put out a protective arm to make sure Isabella doesn't get too close to the road.

The van is moving like the proverbial bat out of hell as it races past us and soars to the crest of the hill.

Just like it did when it ran me off the road.

My mind whirls. Why was that van chasing me? Or, maybe it wasn't chasing me. Maybe he's just one of those drivers that hates bicycles and bike riders. The kind that never want to share the road.

What if. . .

What if he was in a hurry to get home and I was slowing him down?

Maybe bikes were always slowing him down and he decided to finally make a cyclist pay for all those delays. To make *me* pay.

If he uses this road all the time, he must live around here.

"That's what I was thinking, too," says Isabella.

Oh, yeah. She can definitely read my thoughts.

Her eyes widen with realization. "His home has to be somewhere on the other side of that hill!"

I nod. "Or the place where he works. Maybe he was running late."

"Then why was he gunning up the hill again today? Is he always running late?"

"Maybe. Or maybe he's in a hurry to get home because, I don't know, he has to take care of somebody. Or eat supper. Or watch his favorite game show."

I look at the sun.

"It's the same time of day."

"Huh?"

"The sun. It's midafternoon. That's when he ran me off the road."

"More proof that this is his regular route," says Isabella. "The road he takes to and from—wherever he's going."

I realize Isabella and I are starting to sound like detectives, working a case. Which is a good thing.

Maybe the demon driver will run some other poor cyclist off the road.

Maybe *that's* why I'm still here. My death wasn't supposed to happen when it did. It was a random, freak accident. I was in the wrong place at the wrong time. Just like all those dead people we met in the church graveyard. But maybe I can do something to stop the same thing from happening to some other poor kid.

I heard somebody say once that every life has a purpose. Well, maybe every death has one, too. Mine is to track down whoever was driving that black van. To catch a killer. And, given my current state, I know I can do that and not be afraid. Even if my killer is some kind of demented demon.

There's nothing to fear.

Even a psycho killer can't do anything to me now. I'm already dead.

So, who's driving that black van?

It's time to find out.

CHAPTER 46

"WE NEED TO STAKE OUT this location," I tell Isabella. "The next time he flies up the hill, we'll follow him."

"I don't know, Finn. That van was moving kind of fast."

"We can move faster. We've been zipping and zapping all over the place. All we need to do is concentrate on the van. Lock on to it. Stay super focused. Not let our minds wander off to other places and other times. If we stay in that moment, I know we can zoom up the road after him."

I look at the sky and squint at the sun.

"We need to be here tomorrow at this same time," says Isabella, because, you know, that's what I was thinking.

"Exactly."

"You're going to finish your unfinished business."

"Yeah," I say, realizing Isabella might be right. "I guess so. I think I'm supposed to stop that maniac from running some other cyclist off the road. After he killed me, he didn't even turn around to go see what he'd done. He's, basically, a hit-and-run driver. That's a crime. He's a criminal."

Isabella nods. Slowly. I can tell she's thinking. I just can't tell about what. (Maybe you have to be dead as long as she has to pick up that particular superpower.)

"I'm impressed, Finn," she finally says. "What you're going to do is pretty brave."

"Hey, I'm dead. What's there to be afraid of? I just wish I'd felt this way when I was alive."

"Well, maybe you can," says Isabella, "if you get that do-over we were talking about."

"Yeah. Maybe I'll be reincarnated as a very brave cow or something. But here's the hard part: I need to figure out how to tell the police. I'm good with the tracking down part. But, once I know who the guy is and where he lives, what am I supposed to do with that information? Write it all with a frosty fingertip on the windshield of the first cop car we find?"

She grins. "You'll figure it out."

"Christopher would. He's smart. But me?"

"So are you. Finn?"

"Yeah?"

"You're inspiring me."

"Well, I guess there's a first time for everything. . ."

"I'm being serious. What you're doing takes guts."

"Not sure if I actually have any of those anymore. . ."

"Quit kidding around," she says with a small laugh. "Look, if you can be brave, maybe I can be brave, too. I'm ready to go home."

"Seriously?"

"Yeah. It's time. No, it's past time. I need to go see my mother."

CHAPTER 47

I GLANCE UP at the sky again.

"So let's go visit her. We don't need to be back here until this time tomorrow. You're on Oak Street, right?"

"Yes. 48 Oak Street."

She says it and you know the drill. *BOOM!* We're there. Inside the house. There's a beautiful lady in the living room. She is decked out in workout clothes, pumping away on a stationary bike. She has a phone glued to her ear.

"That's my mother," Isabella whispers. "She works out a lot. She's kind of perfect like that."

I can tell Isabella's nervous. Tense. I can hear it in her voice.

"I'm glad you like the piece, Jennifer," Mrs. Rojas says into the phone. "We'll hold it for you. What about the matching earrings? I know. They're absolutely fabulous together. No, a girl can never have too many diamonds. . ."

"She owns a jewelry store," Isabella whispers. "Nothing

Careful, Mrs. Rojas. There might be
a creepy black van behind you.

but high-end stuff. Whatever earrings she's talking about probably cost tens of thousands of dollars."

Her mother keeps pedaling, listening to her caller's question.

"No. She still hasn't come home. But she will. I know Isabella. She was just being dramatic. It's been four months. I'm sure she'll get tired of living with her father soon enough. I know I sure did."

Mrs. Rojas shares a laugh with her caller.

"She didn't really 'run away from home,' Jennifer. I guarantee you, she and her father were in cahoots. My ex can be very sneaky, very clever. I'm sure they planned the whole thing. He probably picked her up that morning on her way to school and whisked her off to Disney World. Took her off the grid to drive me cuckoo. Yes. I hired a private investigator. He's been keeping an eye on Eduardo's house. But Isabella isn't there. My guess? After Disney World he enrolled her in some posh private boarding school in the middle of nowhere. Maybe even registered her under a phony name. Oh, yes, he would. He's very sneaky, Jennifer. Very clever."

I turn to Isabella.

"She doesn't know you're dead?" I say.

"They never found my body. Remember?"

Right. All those "missing child" posters and billboards. Isabella's mother thinks Isabella is still alive.

"Oh, don't worry, Jen," her mom says into the phone. "One way or another, I'll find her. And then I'll have Eduardo arrested for kidnapping! The judge gave me sole custody! I don't care. I'm going to win this thing."

Yikes. It sounds to me like Isabella's mother is more interested in busting Isabella's father than having her daughter safe at home.

"I'm so sorry," I say.

Isabella gives me a feeble smile. "That's my mom for you. It's just the way she is. She's super competitive."

She moves closer and gives her mother a kiss on the cheek.

I can tell that her mom felt it. She shivers a little.

This kiss, though, is kind of sweet.

But then Mrs. Rojas grabs her workout towel and swipes the cheek clean. Like it's too wet from that dribble of cold sweat she just felt.

That's kind of sad.

Isabella turns to face me.

"She has to learn the truth, Finn. She needs to know I'm never coming home. They have to find my body. This is *my* unfinished business and I need to finish it."

I nod. "Okay. I'll help."

CHAPTER 48

"TELL ME WHAT you remember," I say to Isabella.

We're in her backyard, sitting side by side on a rusty swing set—probably left over from when Isabella was little. (I guess if we rock back and forth a tiny bit, passersby will just think the wind is blowing.)

"Shouldn't we concentrate on finding your van driver?" Isabella says.

Yep. She's stalling. Big time.

"My guy won't be back 'til tomorrow—whatever that means since we've been time-leaping all over the place. But it doesn't matter. Right now, I think it's important that we start figuring out what happened to *you*. What do you remember?"

She stares off at something I can't see as she tries to piece together her fragmented memories.

"Okay," she says, sighing like she might as well get this over with. "It was a Friday. Morning. Before school. It was pouring rain. I remember I was wearing my bright-yellow rain slicker. It was supposed to be my weekend with my dad. I only get a few of those every year. Mom had really good divorce lawyers. Anyway, that Friday my father was supposed to pick me up after school. I'd spend the weekend at his place. A condo. It's in the city. But then, Mom got a call. . ."

All of a sudden, we flash back together. I'm with the ghostly Isabella and it's like we're watching a DVR recording of her past. She is on the porch, with her backpack tucked under her rain poncho. There's a faint smile on her lips. I can tell: she's really looking forward to spending some time with her father.

She flips up the hood on her slicker, pops open an umbrella, and scampers down the steps into the pouring rain.

Now her mother comes out onto the covered porch. She's in workout clothes. The kind that cost more than normal clothes. She's also carrying her phone.

"Isabella?" she calls out, because Isabella from the past is all the way down at the sidewalk.

"Yes, Mom?" The Isabella in the scene turns around. She has to scream to be heard in the downpour. Chunky rain-drops are pelting her umbrella.

"Don't listen to anything your father says about me. It's all lies. I don't know why I still let him drive you to school once a month. . ."

Her mother goes back into the house. She's furious and slams the door behind her.

Isabella's phone buzzes.

It's a text from her father's personal assistant.

He won't be driving her to school. They won't be spending the weekend together.

Something "came up."

Isabella is all alone, standing on the sidewalk, in the pouring rain.

The scene fades away. Isabella's eyes are moist. I can tell this is a super painful memory. No wonder she's been blocking it.

"Oh-kay," I say, hoping that I can stick to the facts and avoid all the emotional dynamite. "Your mom and dad definitely won't win any parenting awards. . ."

I'm trying to be funny. It's not working.

I have never seen Isabella's face so pale and ashen. It's like she's in shock.

"He didn't want me," she mutters, still staring at where the image of her mother had been. "*She* didn't want me. Nobody wanted me."

"That's not true," I say, because, I don't know, it sounds like what the school counselor would say in this situation, I guess.

Isabella gives me a look. A real "don't insult me, Finn" look.

"Sorry," I say. "You're right. It sucks. Totally."

"I knew nobody would miss me at school. Except maybe my home room teacher, but only because she has to take attendance every morning. Did you miss me, Finn?"

"Back then? Four months ago?"

She nods.

I have to be honest. "No. I didn't even know who you were until I saw all those missing child posters and billboards."

"Well, don't be too hard on yourself. *Nobody* knew who I was. I was the invisible girl before I became a ghost. Anyway, instead of heading to school that Friday, I decided to run away from home."

"Okay. Where were you going?"

"I don't remember. I may not've had an actual destination. I just knew I wanted to run away."

"Which direction did you head?"

"That way." She points. It's the opposite direction from school. "Downtown. Main Street. The metro bus stop. I had my lunch money. I figured it'd be enough for the fare."

"Where were you going?"

"Anywhere but here."

CHAPTER 49

WE'RE AT THE BUS STOP downtown.

Actually, it's just a gas station with a BUS STOP sign on a pole at the curb.

"The Metro Transit bus goes to St. Paul," I say, because that's the main destination for commuters from our Minnesota town who don't want to (or can't) drive their own cars into the city.

"Like I said, I only had my lunch money," Isabella tells me, her face lined with concentration as she tries to piece together her memory fragments. "So I couldn't afford to go all the way to St. Paul. Besides, I don't know anybody in the city except my father and he wasn't going to be there. So I didn't go to St. Paul. I had enough for a ride to somewhere between here and there. . ."

I look at the route map mounted on the curbside pole. It lists all the stops between this gas station and St. Paul. Luckily, it's not many.

We're finally getting somewhere. The only problem? We have no idea where that somewhere might be.

"Do any of these places ring a bell?" I ask. "Oakdale? Lake Elmo? Route Thirteen?"

"Route Thirteen!" says Isabella. "Yes. There's another gas station. It's in the middle of nowhere but it was close to where I wanted to be."

"Where was that?"

"I don't remember. All I remember is the feeling that I had to go there. That it'd be safe."

"For real?"

"Yes, Finn. The feeling told me where to go. It was a purely emotional decision. I took the bus to the Route Thirteen stop. The gas station had a little shop. I had enough money left over to buy a doughnut. I ate it and waited for the rain to stop. But it didn't. It kept coming down. So, I decided, what the heck. I'd just walk. Something strong was calling to me. Pulling me. Seriously, Finn. I could feel it. If I could get to this place, this place I can't remember, I knew people there would actually want me. I'd be happy."

"Okay. This is good. Maybe you didn't make it to your final destination. Maybe something happened along the way. Something bad. Can you remember where you wanted to be yet?"

She shakes her head. "No. Sorry. That part's still foggy."

"That's okay," I tell her. "We have plenty of time. In fact, we have all the time in the world. An eternity. . ."

"But don't you want to move on?" she says. "After we catch that crazy van driver who ran you off the road, your business will be finished. You won't need to stay here any longer."

"I'm not going anywhere until we find your body and give your parents what they always call 'closure' in the movies. They may not be the best mom and dad in the world but they deserve to know what happened to you, Isabella. So do you. Once you do, maybe you can move on, too. Maybe we can move on together."

"I'd like that. Thanks, Finn."

I try to fit together these first few jigsaw puzzle pieces. Isabella wanted to go to her happy place. The only problem? She can't remember where that place was or is. My guess? Her body is somewhere between that other gas station where she bought the doughnut and her final destination. The place where she'd feel happy.

Now it's my turn to remember something.

"Route Thirteen is at the bottom of the hill. The one where I died. That's where the blinking red light is. That gas station where you got off the bus is pretty close to where I flew off the cliff."

"Maybe. But Route Thirteen is pretty long, Finn. Like ten, twenty miles..."

Suddenly, shadows swing across Main Street as the sun races through the sky like an arcing three-point shot, dunks itself on the western horizon, and plunges us into darkness. Ten seconds later, BAM! It's dawn. Tomorrow. Fresh shadows race across the ground as the big ball of sunshine rises swiftly in the east, crossing over our heads, slowing down.

"It's afternoon again," says Isabella.

I wonder if she pulled the stunt with the sun. Was it a major "let's change the subject, Finn" move?

"We need to be at your roadside memorial," she says.

And just like that, we are.

CHAPTER 50

WE STAKE OUT my roadside memorial, which, come on, people, is now littered with even more fast-food bags and wrappers and cardboard clamshells with moldy orange gunk from last week's cheeseburgers. There's also a peeled-off tire tread. If it was sad before, now it's totally depressing. The stuffed animals all look like wet rats.

"It's almost time," says Isabella.

"Hmm?" I'm distracted. Feeling sorry for myself. Seeing wilted bouquets of dead flowers wrapped in soggy tissue paper at the place where you passed away will do that to you.

"Your van, Finn. It should be coming along any minute now. If he's on the same schedule."

He is.

My black van, the rolling Darth Vader death machine, pulls to a stop at the Route Thirteen blinking light down at the bottom of the hill. We can hear its engine rattling, like it's not firmly bolted in place.

The engine revs.

The crazed lunatic has, once again, jammed the accelerator pedal down to the floor mat. The van belches black smoke and roars up the hill. The engine is straining as the madman makes it move much faster than it wants to. It grinds past us in a blur.

But we chase after it.

Oh, yeah. As predicted, we can do that. We can fly up to the crest of the hill and then zoom down the other side. We're right on its bumper.

Once the van is over the hill, the driver slows down. He starts obeying all the posted speed limits. Guess he doesn't want the police pulling him over and asking him questions about why he likes to chase bicycles off cliffs.

After a mile or so, the driver turns onto a rutted dirt road in the middle of nowhere. The van bounces along through the thick forest, bounding over potholes and the occasional boulder. His rear tires are kicking up all sorts of dust, which is fine by Isabella and me. We don't sneeze anymore.

Finally, the van comes to a stop in what passes for the driveway of a creepy cottage that's seen way better days. It's probably seen better *years*. It's shabby. And lopsided. And dilapidated. What paint is left is crackled and curling, exposing gray wooden clapboards.

The driver, the old man in a trucker cap, climbs out of the van and stretches. He makes his way to a rusty mailbox, creaks it open, and removes a pile of envelopes.

"Nothing but bills and junk mail," the old man mutters. "Bills and junk mail and more junk mail." He takes off the trucker hat to swipe the sweat off his dome. He's bald up top.

Suddenly, something catches his eye.

A soggy foam football snared in a bramble of bushes, a hedge that hasn't been trimmed since the house's most recent paint job (sometime in the last century). He grabs

Ghosts make the best detectives.
We're always undercover.

the spongy ball, which is soaked with grungy rainwater, and heaves it over the hedge. The nasty thing dribbles and wobbles through the air like a water balloon, then lands on the lawn—and I use that term loosely—of the cottage next door. Okay. It's another shack. I was trying to be polite.

He goes to the banged-up green plastic bin at the curb, shuffles through his mail, and tosses several pieces into the pile of recyclable paper. He heads up to the house.

I swoop in to check out the address labels on the discarded mail in the bin. I want to see if I can spy a name.

Some are just addressed to Occupant or Current Resident.

But one is addressed to Mr. Loy Owenby.

Loy Owenby. The name does not mean anything to me but at least I now know the name of the crabby old geezer who killed me.

But I still don't know *why*.

What did Mr. Loy Owenby have against me? I never threw a squishy football into his yard or broke one of his windows with a foul tip.

I need a motive. Some reason for him doing what he did. The police always need a motive in the movies.

So what was Mr. Owenby's?

What was his reason for wanting me dead?

Or was just riding my bike on the same road where he was driving his van reason enough for him to run me off a cliff?

CHAPTER 51

WHEN THE SUN SETS, Isabella and I head back to the Lake.

We love it here. We sit down on the rocks ringing the water. We skip a few stones across the still surface. Good thing nobody else is around. Otherwise, stones magically leap-frogging across the Lake might freak them out.

Skipping stones is one of those things you do when you're trying to think, or, if you're Mickey, trying to show off. He swears he once skimmed a flat rock clear to the other side. "Fourteen bounces!" he said. Of course, no one was there to witness or verify his championship move but, hey, he probably did it. Like I said, the guy is quite the jock.

Isabella and I are quiet. We're both trying to figure things out. What happened to us? Why?

"Are you going to turn Mr. Owenby in to the police?" Isabella finally asks.

"I guess," I say. "But I'd like to know why he did it. Why me?"

"If he really is a psycho, Finn, there may not be a rational reason. Maybe you should let the police figure that part out."

"I guess." I skim another stone. "How about you? Remembering anything after the stop on Route Thirteen?"

She shakes her head. "Nothing. It's like that part of my brain is asleep and won't wake up."

"So," I say with a sly grin, "let's throw some cold water in its face!"

"Excuse me?"

"Let's go for a swim! My friends always said the water here is very refreshing. I'd like to find out what they meant."

"Seriously?"

"Yep. Come on. Let's go for a moonlight swim!"

Isabella blushes a little. "Skinny dipping?"

"Nah. We don't need to worry about our clothes getting wet. We're the Dead Kids, remember? Our clothes are probably waterproof or invisible or, I don't know, not even real. And how can they get wet if they're not really there?"

Isabella laughs and stands beside me. "You make a good point. But I thought you were afraid of the Lake."

"I used to be. My whole life. But, here's another good thing about being dead: we don't have to worry about drowning."

Isabella laughs again. I pinch my nose.

"Um, Finn? Why are you pinching your nose?"

I shrug. "I dunno. It's just something Axe does before he leaps into the water."

"Fine."

Isabella pinches her nose. I count to three. We both hop in.

Okay. The Lake is even more amazing when you're actually in it. It's so cold! So brisk and invigorating. I know this is a strange thing to say, but I've never felt more alive.

I want to swim out to the middle. The spot where everybody says the Lake is bottomless.

"Come on," I say.

Isabella follows me out to the deepest spot. I know where it is. My friends were always daring each other to swim out to it. I was always sitting on the shoreline, worrying about their safety. Tonight? I'm feeling all the feels they felt on those hot summer days. I wonder if any of them ever swam out this far at night? I wish I could tell them how spectacular it is. The stars in the sky are reflected in the still surface of the water. It's like Isabella and I are drifting through our own private galaxy.

Yep. I just conquered a few of my fears. Swimming in the Lake. Talking to a girl who isn't Annie. Hey, better late than never, right?

"So," I say after we've both drifted in silence for a few minutes. "Did a plunge in cold water wake up your brain? Any more memories?"

"Maybe," she says.

I flip over and tread water. She does the same. We're looking right into each other's eyes.

"What?" I ask. "What do you remember?"

"A feeling. A warm feeling. Of being loved. Of being safe. I felt so loved and safe right before whatever happened. . . happened. I knew that where I was going would be a place filled with love."

"So, where is that place?"

"I don't know. I mean, it's right there. . .on the tip of my brain."

She sighs.

"I can't remember."

CHAPTER 52

I'M STARTING TO FEEL like my time is almost through.

I'll be moving on, soon. Isabella has been slowly remembering stuff so, in another day or two, her memory of where she went will come back. I know it will. I'll get a message to the cops. I'm not exactly sure how that will work. Not yet. But, I'll figure it out.

Long story short, our unfinished business is about to get finished.

Before I go, though, I need to have a word with my little brother, Charlie.

I think his name, and just like that, I'm in his room. Isabella didn't travel with me. Guess this needs to be a solo flight.

According to the clock on Charlie's bedside table, it's three a.m. He's sound asleep. I want to tell him something. No, I *need* to tell him something.

I bend down and whisper in his ear.

"Don't make the same mistake I made, little bro. Take some chances. Live your life. Every day is a gift. That's why they call it the present." I wince. "Okay. That was corny. I think I read that on a greeting card but, seriously, Charlie—don't wind up like Mom and Dad. Don't be afraid of everything. Yes, there's bad stuff out there. . .like war and bullies and people slipping and falling in their bathtubs. But there's a lot of good things, too. For instance, pine trees. You ever notice how great they smell? And how about the Lake when the moon's floating on its surface? That is super awesome. Sneak out there some night just to see it. Smell the water, too. Smell everything.

"Man, I wish I could talk to you, Charlie. Anyway, all I really wanted to say is take some chances. Live your life. Don't wait

until you're dead to realize how amazing just waking up every day can be. Don't wind up like me."

Suddenly, Charlie's eyes pop open.

"Finn?" he mutters.

"I'm right here, buddy," I tell him.

Charlie's eyes drift shut. He's fast asleep again.

I hope he heard me.

I hope I made it into his dreams.

CHAPTER 53

IT'S AFTERNOON AGAIN.

Isabella and I are together, up on the cliffs.

School's out for the summer, so of course my friends are hanging out on the rocks. Mickey dives in, Olympic-gold-medalist style. Annie and Christopher leap off feetfirst. Axe pinches his nose and does another lake-draining cannonball. They swim around for a little while.

"Go out to the deep spot!" I shout through cupped hands.

"It's awesome out there!" adds Isabella.

My friends can't hear us. They splash around in the water, have a couple chicken fights, then haul themselves back up to the cliffs, to the sunny rock where they've spread out some towels. It's another spectacular day. They're all shooting the breeze. Laughing.

They're all so. . .alive!

A few minutes later, Christopher and Axe launch into the debate they've been having for years. Pizza or pasta.

Doing nothing is actually doing everything!

"Depends on the sauce," says Christopher.

"And the meat," says Axe. "Toppings or mixed-in. . ."

Soon, they're shooting the bull about YouTube videos. And new shows streaming on Netflix. After that, they'll probably discuss what would be in their individual letters from Hogwarts. Yes, they're nerds. My best nerds forever.

At least back when I was alive.

As the afternoon slips forward, I realize something kind of sad. Kind of shocking.

Nobody mentions me.

Not once.

And we've been eavesdropping on them for hours. Apparently, I'm not just gone. I'm forgotten. Maybe forever.

A group of girls comes over to flirt with Mickey.

"Hey, Mickey," says a girl with dark-brown hair. There are two other girls with her.

"Hey, Maria," he says suavely. "I see you brought some friends. Have you ladies met my main man Axe and my best bro Christopher?"

Maria giggles. Her friends giggle. Axe beams. Annie rolls her eyes. Christopher stares at his shoes.

Isabella grabs hold of my arm. I feel a chill.

"Maria!" she says urgently, like it's the most important name in the universe. "Maria!"

I have no idea why she keeps saying that.

And, unfortunately, I can't focus on her right now.

Because Mickey just invited everybody to grab their bikes and head up Ridge Rim Road to the Tip Top Dairy Barn, this roadside ice cream place we'd go to sometimes for a swirl cone after a hot day at the Lake.

"Ridge Rim Road?" says the girl named Maria. "That's not how you get to Tip Top."

Mickey grins. "It is if you want to get there before the custard melts."

"It's a shortcut," says Axe. "We just discovered it the other day."

"But," cautions Christopher, "you have to pump really hard to make it up that steep hill after the blinking stoplight at the crossroads with Route Thirteen."

I agree. Because that's what I was doing on that very same hill when the maniac ran me off the road.

At four-thirty in the afternoon.

I glance down at Christopher's smartwatch.

It's four-twenty.

I do some quick math.

My friends are going to be biking up the hill on Ridge Rim Road right when Loy Owenby will be heading home to his creepy cottage in his black death van!

CHAPTER 54

MY FRIENDS GRAB their bikes.

The group of girls grabs theirs. Everybody's laughing. One of the girls is showing Annie some dance moves. Mickey's pushing his and Maria's bikes by their handlebars because it makes his biceps, his "guns," bulge. Meanwhile, Isabella is staring off at the horizon repeating the name *Maria*.

"Maria. . ." she mutters.

"We need to stop these guys."

"I'm remembering something, Finn. *Maria*. Why is that name so familiar?"

"We'll figure it out. Later. Right now, we need to stop my friends. They're going to be on the hill when the madman comes racing home. He'll run them all off the road! I know he will."

"How can we stop them?"

"I don't know. There's no glass to write anything on. We could give them the chills!"

"Good idea."

We leap through my friends. They, of course, shiver.

"Oooh," says Mickey. "Just thinking about all that cold and frosty ice cream is giving me goose bumps."

"Me, too," says Axe. "Come on, you guys. If we hurry, we can beat the rush."

"I want a swirl cone," says the girl with the dark-brown hair.

"No problem, Maria," says Mickey.

Which makes Isabella start muttering, "Maria. . .Maria. . ." again.

"YOU GUYS?" I shout. "Forget taking your new shortcut. Just go the normal way. Stay off Ridge Rim Road! Please?"

Whatever worked at my funeral isn't working here. Nobody hears me!

They rattle their bikes down the footpath. Isabella and I hurry along beside them.

"Please." I whisper this directly into Christopher's ear. He's the smart one. The most sensitive one. My best friend. Maybe we can make a psychic connection. "You do not want to take any kind of shortcut, Christopher! You do not want to take the shortcut."

"Is it really a shortcut?" one of the other girls asks Christopher. From the way she asks it, I can tell: she likes Christopher and just wants to find an excuse to talk to him. "Because I'm, like, starving."

"Um, yeah," says Christopher.

"Awesome. You're the best. I'm Mia."

"Christopher." Oh, great. He's looking directly at her. Now he decides to make eye contact? No way will he hear my pleading. Mia has him mesmerized. I think Christopher's falling in love.

"Bad timing," I mutter.

In a flash, they're biking up Ridge Rim Road. A caravan of seven bikes, clustered along the right-hand shoulder of the road. They're taking up a lot of roadway. They will annoy any driver who comes along, especially if it's a grouchy old man.

"Here comes the hill!" shouts Mickey, who's in the lead of the bike pack. "Attack! Attack! Attacky-tack-tack!" He sounds like he's giving a battle cry in an online video game.

Mickey stands up on his pedals and pumps hard. Annie, who's super competitive, tries to pass Mickey on his right.

Isabella and I are floating along with them. I spread out my arms like a crossing guard. Isabella hollers at them.

"You guys? Turn around! This is a mistake. The old man who killed Finn is going to kill you, too."

It doesn't matter. Nothing we can say or do will stop what is about to happen. We've been reduced to nothing more than panicked observers.

And now I hear a familiar rumbling engine.

I look over my shoulder, down the hill. To the blinking stoplight.

Here comes the black van. It's peeling wheels like a drag racer who just got the green light. Loy Owenby is behind the wheel. He didn't wear his trucker hat today. The afternoon sun glints off his shiny bald head. Black fumes are belching out of his tailpipe. The van is moving faster. Faster.

Old man Owenby is going to kill all my friends and the three girls they just met.

He's going to run them all off the road!

We really *are* going to be best nerds forever because we're all going to be dead!

Here we go again. Over the edge and down to the jagged rocks.

CHAPTER 55

THE VAN is twenty yards away from the bikes.

It's struggling up the hill. The engine sounds sick. I feel sick to my stomach. Queasy.

The van rumbles closer to the bikes. Mr. Owenby is gunning his engine. The motor is whining. Straining. The gap narrows between the van and Christopher, who's still at the rear of the pack.

Ten yards.

Five.

"YOU GUYS?!?"

They don't hear me. I close my eyes. I can't stand to see what's going to happen next. The van is going to plow through all seven of them and fling them off Ridge Rim Road. It's going to do to them what it did to me.

And then I hear a "toot-toot."

A jolly horn honk.

I pry open my eyes. The van is moving very, very slowly. Struggling. Stuttering. Like a roller coaster that may. . .not . . .make. . .it. . .all the way up to the top of the first, highest hill on the track.

I look at Mr. Owenby behind the wheel. He has a sheepish grin on his face. Like his clunker of a van is embarrassing him. That he knows it may not make it up and over the hill. When the van is parallel to my friends, the old man shrugs then waves.

"Hey, Mr. Owenby," shouts Maria.

"Howdy, Maria."

"When are you going to buy a new van?"

Mr. Owenby actually laughs. "As soon as I win the lottery. Give my best to your folks."

"Will do. See you at church on Sunday."

"See you then." He gives Maria a brisk, two-finger salute. "If this old rattletrap can make it that far!"

The van reaches the top of the crest—doing about two miles an hour. Gravity takes over on the downhill side and the van picks up speed. So do my friends. The van cruises along while the seven bikes coast downhill, zipping toward the ice cream place. Mickey even kicks out both of his feet and lets the pedals spin in a blur. Maria does the same thing. She adds a "wheeeeee!"

Isabella and I watch them fly down the slope from our viewing post at the top of the hill.

I know exactly what happened the day
I died: I was an idiot.

I'm stunned. Thunderstruck. Gobsmacked.

Suddenly, I totally understand. I know what really happened on the day that I died.

The black van was never chasing me.

The old man wasn't a demonic monster from a Stephen King movie trying to run me off the road. The black van wasn't evil. It was just a gas-guzzling hunk of junk that couldn't handle a steep incline.

Of course Mr. Owenby jammed his pedal to the metal and gunned his engine. He needed to gain as much speed and momentum as possible to make it up and over the hill. He probably never even saw me. He was too focused on urging his rattletrap wreck of a van up the slope.

Turns out, I was afraid of. . .nothing. Owenby was never trying to kill me.

My own fear killed me.

I am an idiot!

CHAPTER 56

I CAN HEAR MY FRIENDS laughing as they coast down the hill for their ice cream.

I return to the memorial. The scene of the crime. My own crime against me. Isabella hovers behind me as I gaze down the hill to the jagged rocks below.

"Fear is the enemy, Isabella," I tell her. "If you're not careful, it can kill you."

"Fear can also keep you alive, Finn."

"True. I guess. Maybe that's why I was wearing my helmet when I went flying over the ledge. A lot of good it did me. . ."

"Maybe we need both," says Isabella. "Fear and courage. A balance."

I nod. "Sounds like a plan. Wish I had learned it while I was alive."

"Yeah. Me, too. I was afraid of everything and everybody. Except Maria."

Uh, yeah. I've been sort of focused on me, me, me. I'd almost forgotten about Isabella and the lightbulb that popped on over her head when she heard the name *Maria*. My business is finished. Done. It's time to focus on finishing hers. Then, we can both move on. Am I afraid of what might come next? Maybe. A little bit. But, lesson learned. I am not going to let fear rule or ruin my life. I mean my afterlife.

"So who's Maria?" I ask.

"My aunt!" she says, her eyes brighter than I've ever seen them. "It all came back to me. While we were on the hill and your friends were talking about taking a shortcut. That's what I did, I think. I mean I'm pretty sure. I took a shortcut. A shortcut, Finn! That's the answer."

Isabella is so animated, I almost forget that she's dead. She's so full of life and happiness that it makes me happy.

I kind of wish I had known this Isabella when she and I were both alive. She would've fit in with my crew. Definitely. I'm liking her more and more. Have we reached full-on romantic crush level? Not important. Probably impossible given our, you know, situation.

"So," I say, "tell me about your Aunt Maria."

"She's my father's sister. She always calls me Izzy."

"Really?"

"Yeah. It's short for Isabella."

"Izzy. I like it. It's, I don't know, more fun."

"Exactly, Finn! That's Aunt Maria. She was the total opposite of my mom and dad. I actually laughed when I would spend the night at her house. We'd watch silly movies. Scary ones, too. We'd make a big bowl of popcorn. I know it doesn't sound like much but we never had popcorn at my house, before or after the divorce. Popcorn is messy. And fattening. And noisy. When I was at Aunt Maria's, I could be messy and noisy and just be myself. I could be the me I liked a whole lot better than the me I had to be at home in the Perfect Palace."

"So where does your Aunt Maria live?"

"Near Route Thirteen, I think."

"You think?"

"That part is still hazy. I remember her. I remember her laugh. Her dog. Her two cats. Her big purple bowl for popcorn. The way her kitchen always smelled like she'd just baked cookies. . ."

"And the street address?"

Isabella shakes her head. "That's where I draw a blank."

"That's okay. We'll find it. It'll come to you."

I realize how inconvenient it is to be stuck in this limbo without Google or a GPS map app. There is no Wi-Fi or high-speed internet when you're dead.

"I took a shortcut," Isabella says. "From that gas station to Aunt Maria's. I wanted to get there as quickly as I could. Plus

it was raining. I didn't want to get totally soaked. So. . .yes
. . .I cut through the woods."

"The forest alongside Route Thirteen?"

Once again, Isabella is staring at something nobody else can see as she tries to remember her last day on earth. Well, the last alive one, anyway.

"Yes! I remember now. I remember everything!"

CHAPTER 57

WHEN ISABELLA says she remembers everything she actually means "almost everything."

"I walked out of the gas station," she says.

My job is to say "uh-huh" and nod to keep her memory stream flowing.

"It was raining. Pouring. I was wearing my yellow rain slicker."

"Uh-huh."

"I went up Route Thirteen maybe half a mile. My shoes were soaked. My socks were squishy."

I nod.

"I realized I'd probably die of pneumonia if I hiked the five miles to Aunt Maria's house. So, I checked my phone. The map app. If I went on the diagonal, cut through the woods, it'd only be a mile, maybe two..."

"Do you remember *where* you got off Route Thirteen?" I ask. "Where you went into the woods?"

"No. But I had my map app up and running. At least until I lost signal. I knew I needed to keep heading downhill and I'd end up in her backyard. Right there at 102 Whippoorwill Lane."

Her eyes bulge.

"Ohmigod. I just remembered her address! 102 Whippoorwill Lane. That's where Aunt Maria lives! It's a cute house. What she calls a Craftsman cottage. There's a porch swing out front. If I was going to run away from home for good that was the home I wanted to run away to!"

"Okay," I say. "This is excellent. We have the gas station on Route Thirteen and the cottage at 102 Whippoorwill Lane. What happened in between?"

"I was in the woods. My phone stopped working. There wasn't any signal. I guess you could say I was lost because I had no idea where I was, just where I wanted to be. I wondered if I was walking around in circles because I kept seeing this same moss-speckled rock. I panicked. I started running. It was still raining. The leaves on the ground were wet. I slipped. . ."

She gasps. I wait.

"There was a cliff, Finn. A ledge. I slid, lost my footing, the ground disappeared. I tumbled over the ledge. Just like you did. Only I wasn't on a bike or wearing a helmet. I'm pretty sure I blacked out before I hit the jagged rocks fifty feet below."

Yep. We have something else in common besides being

dead. Falling off a cliff and landing on jagged rocks. Can't forget the jagged rocks.

"I didn't feel any pain," she says. "I just died, I guess. The next thing I knew, I was back at school. Wandering around in that courtyard garden with the butterfly feeders where you saw me all those months later."

"So you just hung around the school? For four months?"

She nods. "Yeah. Mostly. Your fear ran you off the road. Mine kept me stuck at school. And, as you've discovered, time really has no meaning for us."

True. Four months for the two of us could go by in the flap of a few butterfly wings.

"Every once in a while," Isabella continues, "I'd wander off to that graveyard I showed you. I was hoping I might meet some relatives who could tell me what was going on. I didn't. But I did make a few friends. None of them as good as you, though."

"Thanks."

"Some of the spirits at the cemetery would ask me for my story but I couldn't remember much of what had happened to me. Just that I was afraid. I knew my mother would be mad at me. My father, too. Especially after I saw those missing child flyers they hung up at school. I heard kids talking about billboards, too. Were there milk cartons?"

I nod. "You were everywhere, Izzy. For like a week or two. . ."

And then everybody moved on. Just like they did with my roadside memorial.

Lovely day for a walk in the woods. Not!

"All I knew is that I could never go home or say good-bye," Isabella tells me.

"Why not?"

"I was too terrified. I couldn't face my mother. Not even dead. Not after what I had done—even though I couldn't remember what I did. I mean, I went out and died. I ruined her perfect life. People probably came by the house with casseroles and condolences, and my mother doesn't like anybody feeling sorry for her. I think that's why she refuses to accept the fact that I'm dead. Why she thinks I'm in some top secret boarding school or having fun at Disney World with my dad. It's time, Finn. She needs to learn the truth. My father, too. Everybody who tried to find me. We have to let them all know that I'm dead. If we can do that, I think I can move on."

"So, someone has to find your body."

"Correct."

"Somewhere in the woods between that gas station and your Aunt Maria's house."

"Yeah."

"That's a lot of acres of forest."

"I know."

"A whole lot."

"Yeah."

"Okay. I have an idea. . ."

I tell my idea to Isabella. She likes it.

We're going to do this thing.

We're going to finish her unfinished business.

CHAPTER 58

REMEMBER THAT TIME I got airsick flying in the traffic helicopter with Christopher's mother?

Not my best day and probably the first time anybody's puked at a birthday party *before* the cake and ice cream were served. Well, as you also might recall, Mrs. Owens was the one who discovered my body lying in a ravine. It's time for her eye-in-the-sky to find one more.

During the evening rush hour, Isabella and I just think about being inside the WROL traffic chopper and we are. It's early summer, so the sun still has a bunch more hours to go before it ducks down behind the horizon for the night.

I am looking down at the snarled traffic clogging the downtown highways like one of those drug commercials on TV showing cheese or whatever blocking somebody's arteries.

And guess what? I'm not afraid this time. Yes, I'm up in the air without a parachute, but Mrs. Owens is a military-trained pilot. Her helicopter gets regular maintenance and inspections. The controls look very computerized and brand new.

Plus, I'm already dead. What's there to be afraid of?

As Isabella and I look on, Mrs. Owens does her standard spiel about rubbernecking delays and fender benders on all the major roads leading out of town.

I start whispering course corrections.

"Fly up Route Thirteen," I tell her. "Hover over the forest. Forget about traffic. There's bigger news out in the woods."

Mrs. Owens keeps the whirlybird circling over a jack-knifed tractor trailer on the Interstate.

I try again. "Head up Route Thirteen," I whisper. I'm really doing my best to sound spooky, too. Like if a Ouija board could talk.

Isabella joins in. "Hover over the forest."

"Forget about the traffic!" we both whisper together.

"There's bigger news out in the woods!" I tell her. Again.

We get zip in response. Just some more hovering over that poor tractor trailer lying on its side on the shoulder of the road, leaking cargo. Apparently, this particular eighteen-wheeler was hauling several tons of bananas. They're mashed all over the highway like a yellow oil slick.

I realize whispering isn't going to work. Especially in a helicopter. The whirring blades over our heads make all sorts of thump-thump-thumping noises. It's so loud, Mrs. Owens has to wear super-thick headphones.

Yes, the shouting is all we have left!

So I try screaming.

"FLY UP ROUTE THIRTEEN!" I shout. "HEAD INTO THE FOREST! PLEASE, MRS. OWENS? *PLEASE?*"

Mrs. Owens gets a look on her face. Did she hear me? Is "please" really the magic word everybody always says it is?

"This is chopper one," she says into her head mic. "Stay away from Six-Ninety-Four, unless you love banana splits. Your next traffic report will be coming up in ten minutes, on the twos! Back to you, Brian."

She slides her control stick to the right. We veer off the interstate.

We're heading for Route Thirteen!

Somehow she heard us.

CHAPTER 59

THERE ARE A LOT OF TREES in this forest.

A lot of green leafy trees with big bushy crowns that make it impossible to see much besides trees and more trees.

This was a dumb idea, I think.

"No, Finn," says Isabella, reading my mind. "It was a good idea. It's the best way to search this much territory. I think this was a genius idea."

"But she can't see anything."

We're tracking above the wooded acres alongside Route Thirteen. I can still see the ribbon of asphalt coursing through the greenery. A car or two. But nothing else.

I check out Mrs. Owens's face. Her eyebrows are down. Her gaze is locked on the scene below. Somehow, she heard our thoughts (and she's not even dead like Izzy). Somehow, she knows she's on a search and rescue mission.

Actually, I think, *it's more of a search and recover mission. . .*

And that's when Mrs. Owens gasps and says something

she probably wouldn't've said if she knew there were two dead kids in the chopper cockpit with her.

She brings the traffic helicopter down a few hundred feet. Fast. She's locked on to something. She has a target.

We're hovering right above a slight clearing. A craggy, gray ravine strewn with boulders. I can see a big, jagged hole gouged into the earth with a pool of oily green water in its basin.

And a bright yellow rain slicker.

A body is floating, facedown, in the shallow pond of rain runoff.

"That's my raincoat," whispers Isabella. "That's me!"

We have found her body. Right below the rocky outcropping where she slipped and fell.

"Base?" Mrs. Owens says into her helmet's mic. "We have a situation. Do you have my location? Good. Call nine-one-one. We need a search and recovery team. No, this does not look like a rescue situation. . ."

Mrs. Owens tells her base what she knows. A body. Probably dead. Floating in a shallow pool of murky water. Yellow rain slicker. She is very professional and doesn't launch into any kind of rant about all the dead bodies she's been discovering lately when she's just supposed to be up in the air reporting on the traffic.

"Don't look," I tell Isabella. "You don't want to see this. It

won't be pretty. Don't look. Your business is done. Finished.
This is as far as we need to go."

Isabella closes her eyes.

"I wish you had been my friend back then, Finn," she says
softly.

"Yeah. Me, too."

"You might've talked me out of taking that shortcut. . . ."

"Yeah. I might've. Taking shortcuts through the woods
can be very dangerous. I could probably have told you some of
my dad's statistics about the dangers of hiking and camping

and doing anything remotely woodsy. Or I just could've told you about Hansel and Gretel and what happened to them when they went for a walk in the woods. Little Red Riding Hood, too. . ."

Isabella smiles. Just a little. She even gives me a hint of a laugh. "I'm glad we're friends now, Finn."

"Me, too, Izzy. You ready to move on?"

"Yes. If you don't think it'll be too dangerous."

I shake my head. "Nah. From here on out, there's absolutely nothing left to be afraid of."

CHAPTER 60

WE GO TO MY HOUSE.

I'm pretty sure this will be my last visit. It's just a feeling, but a strong one.

"Good-bye, house," I say when we're standing out front. "Good-bye, lawn. I'll actually miss mowing you. So long, flowers. Mom always made sure there were new ones popping up every season."

We move through the walls. I say good-bye to more stuff. The living room window where we put up our Christmas tree. The dining room where we had dinner every night at five-thirty. It's kind of goofy to be saying good-bye to things. Inanimate objects. But they were all part of my everyday life even though I never really appreciated that life every day.

Now comes the hard part.

Saying good-bye to Mom, Dad, and Charlie.

I give Charlie a hug first. He doesn't shiver. He makes a cozy murmur. The way you do when you feel warm and toasty snuggled underneath the covers on a cold winter night. My good-bye embrace is warming, not chilling.

"Take care of yourself, little man," I tell him. "And take a few risks. Nothing, you know, ridiculous, but get out there a little. At least more than I did."

I find Mom in the kitchen. She's sniffling. Looking at my last class picture. I give her a hug and I know she feels it.

"Finn, you will always be here, in my heart," she tells the photo. She gives my five-by-seven a gentle kiss. I give her one on the cheek. I think she felt that, too.

Finally, I go into the den where Dad is at his desk, crunching numbers on the computer.

"I understand, Dad," I tell him, remembering what I learned from the soldier in the cemetery. "You did your best. You had enough danger and excitement when you were deployed overseas. So you tried to keep us safe from all harm, even though you already knew that it would be an impossible task. Random things happen. Things numbers and statistics just can't predict. I'm sorry about what I did. I let my fears chase me off that cliff. That's not on you, Dad. That's on me. And know that if I had a chance to do things differently, I would. I wouldn't be so afraid. I wouldn't let fear be the thing that told me what to do."

I give him his hug. He sighs and stops clacking on the keyboard. A tear slips out of his eye. Mine, too.

"Okay," I say to Isabella, who's been silently observing my final tour around my home. "I'm done. We need to go to your house."

She nods.

And we're there.

CHAPTER 61

* * * * * * * * * *

ISABELLA'S HOUSE is empty.

She isn't saying good-bye to any of the expensive things artfully arranged around the spacious, white-carpeted rooms.

I realize that, unlike my home, Isabella doesn't have a lot of happy memories associated with this particular place. Maybe we should've gone to her Aunt Maria's. She could've said good-bye to her purple popcorn bowl and that oven where all those cookies got baked.

The door opens. Her mother steps into the foyer and peels off her high-heeled shoes. She places them neatly on the floor and pads across the room, working the clasps on her earrings. They're huge diamonds. She opens a framed painting as if it were a cabinet door to reveal a wall safe. That's where the diamonds will be spending the night.

Isabella looks timid. Maybe even scared.

So I step forward and whisper into her mother's ear.

"Isabella's gone. Isabella's gone. Isabella's. Gone."

A tiny flicker of emotion twitches across her mother's lips. She leaves the living room, heads up the hall, and stops in front of a bedroom door decorated by a single, silver letter *I*. Isabella's room.

She slowly opens the door.

"This is her first time visiting my room since that morning," says Isabella.

"You don't know that for sure. . ." I say quietly, trying to soften the blow.

"Yes, Finn. I do."

Her mother steps into Isabella's room. Sees the stuffed unicorn snuggled between the pillows.

And she begins to cry.

"Oh, my sweet baby," she sobs. "Oh, my sweet, sweet baby. Isabella's gone. And she's never coming back."

The doorbell rings.

Two somber police officers are at the front door, holding their hats in their hands.

We know what they're here to tell Mrs. Rojas.

We don't need to stick around to hear it.

CHAPTER 62

THAT NIGHT, with our business as finished as it's ever going to be, we head back to the Lake.

We stand on the rocks and look at all the twinkling stars in the sky. The moon is up there, too. Smiling.

"We did it," says Isabella with relief. "We said our good-byes. We learned the truth."

I creep forward, right to the ledge of the cliff. The Lake is a shimmering mirror, looking like a second night sky filled with its own bright moon and more stars than anyone could ever imagine.

"I've never jumped off the rocks," I tell Isabella. "I watched my friends do it a billion times. But I never did it myself."

"Because you were afraid?"

"Yeah. I was afraid of drowning. Of what my dad might say if he found out. I was even afraid that I'd lose my bathing suit when I hit the water."

Isabella laughs.

"Hey," I tell her. "I've seen it happen. Axe forgot to button his top button once. He dove and hit the water hard. His trunks went under, popped up on an air bubble, and drifted over to the shore where Mickey snagged them with a stick and wouldn't give 'em back."

Isabella laughs harder. I'm laughing along with her now.

"I always wanted to jump in, though," I tell her. "From way up here—not just down on the shore like we did last time."

"I always wanted to have a friend," says Isabella. "Someone my own age that I could talk to about stuff. Good stuff. Bad stuff. Whatever."

"Well," I say, offering her my hand. "You've got a friend now."

"I know," she says, taking my hand and giving me her genuine Izzy smile. Her hand is soft and warm. Not in the least bit chilly. "And, guess what, Finn? You still have a chance."

"A chance? To do what?"

She nods down to the sparkling lake rippling twenty yards below. "To take the high jump."

"I don't know. . ."

"Yes, you do."

"But it's late. The water will be cold. And it's dark. What if we see a rock or boulder jutting out on the way down?"

"There are no rocks or boulders jutting out, Finn. Just look."

I bend a little, peer over the edge, and try to examine the face of the cliff. I nearly lose my balance. Good thing Isabella is still holding on to my hand. She helps me steady myself and stand up straight. And she's right about the rocks. There's nothing to be afraid of, I realize.

I take it all in, one last time. The smell of the trees. The annoying chirps of the frogs. The white-capped water, lit by the moon, cascading over the rocks and sending up a misty smell that's so crisp, fresh, and clean. It's like I can taste that tumbling water just from its smell. The Lake really is the most spectacular place on a pretty spectacular planet.

"You okay?" Izzy asks.

"Yeah."

"Don't worry. I'll be right beside you—the whole way down."

"Promise?"

"Cross my heart and hope to die."

We both laugh a little at that.

"Ah, what the heck," I say. "Let's go jump in a lake."

I back up from the ledge.

"Uh, Finn? The Lake is down there."

"I know. I just want to get a running start. If we're going to do this thing, let's do it right!"

"Sounds good to me."

We back up about fifteen paces.

We're still holding hands. We tighten our grips.

I turn to Izzy. "To life," I tell her.

"To life!"

We both run as fast as we can to the edge and leap off.

Halfway down, we disappear.

EPILOGUE

* * * * * * * * *

THE FIRST THING Finn McAllister sees when he finally wakes up is the shiny grid of a fluorescent light fixture in the ceiling.

He hears a steady beeping. The hum and whoosh of medical machinery.

He turns his head. It really hurts. He sees his father sitting in a chair close to his hospital bed. His father is weeping.

His father never weeps.

"Dad?" Finn croaks, his mouth dry.

"Finn!" His father springs out of the chair and tries to hug him without disconnecting all the tubes and wires snaking into his body.

Finn smiles.

"You're back!" is all his dad can say because he's sobbing so much. "Thank god, you're back."

Finn nods as best he can. The corners of his eyes feel warm. Tears are welling up in them.

He can't wait to go home. To see his mom and Charlie.

He doesn't have to wait long. His mother and brother burst through the door.

"He's back?" his mother gasps, her hands covering her heart.

"He's back!" says Finn's father through his flood of happy tears.

"Hiya, Charlie," is all Finn is able to say. His voice is so weak.

His little brother rushes across the room and practically crawls into the hospital bed with him to give him a good hug. Finn gives his little brother the same speech he gave Charlie in whatever kind of coma dream he just had in the hospital: *Don't make the same mistake I made, little bro. Take some chances. Live your life. Every day is a gift.*

There's movement at the door. It catches Finn's eye.

A dark-haired girl in a candy-striped volunteer uniform is peeking into the room and smiling. She might be crying, too.

Finn recognizes her.

No.

It couldn't be.

Izzy?

GET YOUR PAWS ON THE HILARIOUS DOG DIARIES SERIES!

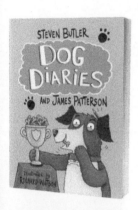

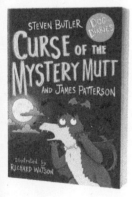

ALSO BY JAMES PATTERSON

MIDDLE SCHOOL BOOKS

The Worst Years of My Life (*with Chris Tebbetts*)
Get Me Out of Here! (*with Chris Tebbetts*)
My Brother Is a Big, Fat Liar
(*with Lisa Papademetriou*)
How I Survived Bullies, Broccoli, and
Snake Hill (*with Chris Tebbetts*)
Ultimate Showdown (*with Julia Bergen*)
Save Rafe! (*with Chris Tebbetts*)
Just My Rotten Luck (*with Chris Tebbetts*)
Dog's Best Friend (*with Chris Tebbetts*)
Escape to Australia (*with Martin Chatterton*)
From Hero to Zero (*with Chris Tebbetts*)
Born to Rock (*with Chris Tebbetts*)
Master of Disaster (*with Chris Tebbetts*)
Field Trip Fiasco (*with Martin Chatterton*)

DOG DIARIES SERIES

Dog Diaries (*with Steven Butler*)
Happy Howlidays! (*with Steven Butler*)
Mission Impawsible (*with Steven Butler*)
Curse of the Mystery Mutt (*with Steven Butler*)
Camping Chaos! (*with Steven Butler*)
Dinosaur Disaster! (*with Steven Butler*)

THE I FUNNY SERIES

I Funny (*with Chris Grabenstein*)
I Even Funnier (*with Chris Grabenstein*)
I Totally Funniest (*with Chris Grabenstein*)
I Funny TV (*with Chris Grabenstein*)
School of Laughs (*with Chris Grabenstein*)
The Nerdiest, Wimpiest, Dorkiest I Funny Ever
(*with Chris Grabenstein*)

MAX EINSTEIN SERIES
The Genius Experiment (*with Chris Grabenstein*)
Rebels with a Cause (*with Chris Grabenstein*)
Saves the Future (*with Chris Grabenstein*)

TREASURE HUNTERS SERIES
Treasure Hunters (*with Chris Grabenstein*)
Danger Down the Nile (*with Chris Grabenstein*)
Secret of the Forbidden City (*with Chris Grabenstein*)
Peril at the Top of the World (*with Chris Grabenstein*)
Quest for the City of Gold (*with Chris Grabenstein*)
All-American Adventure (*with Chris Grabenstein*)
The Plunder Down Under (*with Chris Grabenstein*)

HOUSE OF ROBOTS SERIES
House of Robots (*with Chris Grabenstein*)
Robots Go Wild! (*with Chris Grabenstein*)
Robot Revolution (*with Chris Grabenstein*)

JACKY HA-HA SERIES
Jacky Ha-Ha (*with Chris Grabenstein*)
My Life is a Joke (*with Chris Grabenstein*)

For more information about James Patterson's novels,
visit www.penguin.co.uk